The Secret of the Diamond Ring

Kyle A. Hamer

I S B N   978-0-6152-1392-7

To everyone who helped me in the writing process, and mostly my parents, my cousin Dylan, and my 4th grade teacher Mrs. Beaullieu

The Secret of the Diamond Ring

When a millionaire goes missing, the Hamer Boys chase after the culprit. Amas, the enemy, takes over Maine and steals 19 stores, builds 41 robots, leads 9 gang members, and destruction and distraction. Find out how in this Hamer Boys edition: The Secret of the Diamond Ring!

CONTENTS

KYLE

I've kinda got a sixth sense about mysteries. So see how this one goes. Dylan and I were watching the 7:00 to 9:00 a.m. news while we were cooking pancakes. Marty Lopez was also there. At 8:15, the news talked about a missing millionaire. The newsman reported that nobody knows his name.

"Wow, a missing millionaire!" Dylan exclaimed.

"Let's go investigate for clues." I suggested.

Dylan and Marty didn't find anything but I found a number code that looked like this: 10125141171745 1214...

"That's too bad we didn't bring Dad's codebook." I sighed. "Ask before you speak." Dylan replied and held up the codebook. Here's what the code looked like:

A	B	C	D	E	F	G	H	I	J	K	L	M
1	2	6	5	4	3	7	8	12	11	10	9	13

N	O	P	Q	R	S	T	U	V	W	X	Y	Z
14	18	17	16	15	19	20	24	23	22	21	25	26

After thinking, Dylan said. " Kidnapped in a weird cave called Caribbean Sea Cave on the edge of Madawaska, Maine. HELP! Albert and sons."

"We search today!" I said.

Dylan asked, "The only question is who and why they're capturing that someone."

"I'm calling Dad." I said immediately.

On the phone, I told him about the code and its answer. When I hung up, Dylan asked if I had brought a world map with me.

"Yep." I replied. While in Montana he thought of the Sleuth in Bayport. The map said SR 726.66 statute miles SW and 1,313.97 statute miles SE (AIR FLIGHT) would be 3 weeks, and 3 days.

Through Minnesota, Wisconsin, Illinois, Indiana, Ohio, West Virginia, Pennsylvania, and finally into Bayport, New York. When they got to the boathouse, they were just in time to hear beep, beep, beep, beep from their two-way radio on their boat, "The Detective". Albert Hamer was on the line.

"Calling Dylan and Kyle." he called.

"Calling Albert Hamer. Loud and clear." I called back.

"There are some strange happenings at the house. By the way where are you?"

"In fact, we are in Bayport." I answered.

"I thought you brought the boat." Albert said.

"We ended up not going on the boat." I replied.

"Come home quick!" Aunt Denise shouted.

"I'd love to." Marty said hungry and dazed.

"I'd recognize that voice anywhere!" Aunt Denise and Albert Hamer said, "Marty. Bye. Bye." and hung up. When they got home, Aunt Denise already had dinner ready. They were discussing the case at dinner. While eating Dylan and I spotted a man fleeing across the driveway.

"Excuuuuuse us!" the boys said together. The boys ran after the fleeing man. Dylan got a good glimpse of the man. Meanwhile, I fled to his car and I remembered the license: ENS815Y.

But Dylan wasn't fast enough to catch the man. As he stumbled over a branch and knocked himself unconscious, the man was getting into the car and driving off. As Dylan gained consciousness, he also gained power, strength, and memory.

Dylan also overheard me say, "I have his license number."

I know that because he came up and said, "And I tried to capture the thief but stumbled over a stick accidentally."

"Glad you're up, sleepyhead." I said, "It's been hours already." Dylan looked out of the window of their father's study. It was morning.

"And you didn't have the rest of your dinner. So Aunt Denise scheduled for you to have double the breakfast." I finished.

"That solves my problem." Dylan said, "But what'll be double?"

"Anything you want will automatically be doubled." I explained.

"Tripled." Aunt Denise called from a distance.

"Tripled." I repeated, talking to Dylan and also correcting myself. After that, Dylan went straight to their Dad's study. He looked at some pictures in a drawer.

He left the study and called to me, "Kyle, where did you put the phone book?"

"I put the phone book in the living room on top of the table, Dylan." Dylan looked there. He came on the scene.

"I know I put it there." I said.

"Very funny." Dylan said. I announced that I had put it there again.

"Somebody must have stolen it." Dylan guessed afterwards.

"But why would they need a phone book, Dylan? A phone book is a book that contains addresses and phone numbers."

"Exactly, Kyle. You see, Kyle, addresses help people get where they want to get. Also a phone book can tell you where a house is --" said Dylan when I interrupted with, "and we had a U.S.A. phone book!"

"That means that whoever the gang is that they can go or call whenever they want!" Dylan blurted out.

"Also that means that we cannot go or call anyone that we do not know the address to." I added.

"Wait, Dylan, he may have dropped the phone book accidentally and did not notice it was gone."

"Well I guess we'll have to postpone our search until tomorrow." I sighed.

"Kyle, we can switch 'em. We can go looking for the missing millionaire today, and chase the man tomorrow." Dylan suggested.

"Okay." I said.

They took a car through Massachusetts, Vermont, and into Madawaska, Maine. They had finally found out that it took 1949.7 miles, which took 1 day, 4 hours, and 59 minutes, so it would take about 3 weeks, 6 days, and 30 minutes.

Their car was in the repair garage, being fixed from damage that happened while driving throughout the city. I hailed for a taxi.

Dylan directed him to the Madawaska Repair Garage. The taxi driver drove until the boys saw a sign written in bold print: MADAWASKA REPAIR GARAGE. The man told the boys that the convertible was fixed. I studied 'Madawaska'. I thought and looked at the sign.

3

"That's it! The missing millionaire's name is AKSAW ADAM! The boys went to a hotel.

"May I borrow your phone book?" I asked.

"Sure!" the man replied.

I looked at 'ADAM' and no luck. Wait. Maybe it's ADAM AKSAW. I tried 'AKSAW' and this time had luck. I scrolled down the list. AARON, ABLEST, ACAM, ACE, ADAL, and finally, ADAM!

I looked through the business section in the phone book under the letter "U" and he found U.S.A. News Reporter. The number was (800)-241-9145. I dialed: (800)-241-9145. He reported that this was Kyle Hamer, and elated that he knew his name was Adam Aksaw.

The newswoman told the whole United States of America, so everyone knows his name: Adam Aksaw.

After unscrambling and referring to the phone book, I said loudly, "AMAS KAWDA!"

The address was 396 Jamaame Dr. in Africa. From Maine into "The Detective", our boat, across the Atlantic Ocean, back in the car, France, Spain, in "The Detective", again, Atlantic Ocean, back in the car Morocco, Algeria, Sudan, and into Ethiopia, and Mogadishu, and into Jamaame. They checked into a hotel.

"Room 2000." the man said. There was a terrace in their room.

"Let's have some chow." Marty said.

"Well, we'll have to get our own food. It's 4:00 in the morning." I stated.

"Not even breakfast, yet. Humph." Marty moaned.

"Maybe a morning swim will take your mind off of your hunger." I suggested.

" Maybe a morning swim will take your mind off of your hunger." Marty mocked him as to start an argument.

"Excuse me!" I said in a high pitch voice. "I was just trying to make a suggestion." he said in a lower-pitch sound.

"Well, you think a mor-- " Marty said, but Dylan interrupted, "Break it up! One at a time, elaborate what happened so I can settle it, or else, for pete's sake!"

"Well, Marty started mocking me when I asked him about a morning swim." I started.

"He knows that a boring swim doesn't do any good for my appetite." Marty said.

"Kyle, Marty's right. Marty, do not mock Kyle." Dylan articulated. The boys found a key, and chest that had just appeared suddenly, and put the key in the lock, and had no luck.

"Can we just get onto 386 Jamaame Dr.?" I begged.

"I have no choice but to agree." Striding along the road, the boys spotted Jamaame Dr..

"There is no 386!" I announced excitedly! "380, 382, 384, 388! "It was a-- there was a pause-- phony address!" Dylan said weirdly. The boys did not recognize it read 396 not 386.

"Let's go back to that man with the phone book." Dylan said angrily.

I looked at my watch, and whispered to Dylan, "No, not now because it's 6:00 p.m., and Chet will be upset if we don't go eat breakfast now."

The three boys went to a restaurant, and ate. Afterwards, the three boys went to the hotel. Dylan called his father to tell him about of the case.

Here's what he told him: "Dad, we're having a lot of angles to the case. You -- Albert interrupted as if not listening-- "I heard there is a key auction there. Would you like to go?" Dylan's face lit with glee.

"Dad, we need to go there. We found a key, and a chest. We put the key in the rusted lock, and had no luck."

"Well, you should be able to go. Kyle has a large sum of 1 million dollars, from mystery-solving, you know." Albert Hamer said.

"Okay, bye." they said together.

Dylan came to me and said, "You kept a secret from me. Dad said you had $1 million dollars."

"Whoa!" Marty said.

"Also, dad said that there's a key auction here." Dylan added.

"So we can use my 1 million dollars to buy the keys at the auction!" I said happily.

"Or you can replace the millionaire yourself!" Marty teased and laughed.

" For me to be that millionaire I'd have to have 26,000,000 more dollars." Kyle said.

"And to beat the richest person ever he'd have to have at least 93,000,000 to 99,000,000 more." Dylan added.

"Then let me go 2 times. 1st is that the richest person you're thinking has 93,000,000. 2nd is that if a hamburger is 65 cents, you could buy 15,384 of them and have nothing left." Marty said.

I said, "In fact Dylan has $550,000, and you have?" "$473,586 and 50 cents." Marty answered.

"So in all we have $2,023,586 and 50 cents." I said immediately after some quick addition.

"Now we can buy 31,132 hamburgers and have ten cents left!" Marty explained.

Two days later driving for breakfast I saw a sign saying: MADAWASKA KEY AUCTION: TODAY AT 5:45 PM AT MADAWASKA'S DANCING STAGE.

At 5:45 the boys went to the auction. The boys got two of the keys. None of them worked on the chest.

"We have to get that key!" Dylan said angrily.

"Awwww. We could have afforded stocks of food with that!" Marty slumped onto the floor.

"Uhh… Marty…?" Marty glanced up at me. I held a check for two million, twenty-three thousand four hundred thirty dollars.

"We only spent a mere $186."

"Why don't we call the others like Mary, Kim, Roger, Bobby, and your dad." Dylan suggested. Bobby, Roger, Kim, and Mary sometimes helped on cases and were pretty good detectives.

"I've got their phone numbers." Marty continued. I dialed 459-6377, 473-8655, 647-8746, and 744-6780 to see if they could help without telling Aunt Denise.

Marty blurted out," I've found it! The key! It was under the couch and I found it!" The key worked! Nothing was in the chest.

"Let's soak it and pull the felt out." I suggested. Next thing they knew they were staring at a diamond ring!

"We'd- bet- ter -bring- this- to- the-pol- ice- head- quar- ters." Dylan stammered. The boys closed the chest and set off to police headquarters as Marty headed for home. They showed Chief Besmal the find.

"I didn't know this thing was about a diamond ring, too." Chief Besmal reported.

"Too? You mean there's more than we know!" I said.

"Yep." Chief Besmal replied.

"Tell us then. We need to know any information." Dylan stated.

"Well, first of all there's a bunch of burglaries." Chief Besmal said.

"We'll need a list of those." I said.

"Secondly, and lastly, vandalism's been going on." Chief Besmal continued.

The list read:

1. Aunt Sally's Fried Chicken
2. Uncle Bob's Auto Shop
3. Service Merchandise
4. Price Low
5. Del Champs
6. William's Jewelry
7. The Door Store
8. The Bell Farm
9. The Pizza Place
10. African Artifacts Museum and more from A-Z

"The lead person or persons must have a gang." Dylan said.

"There's a paper attached." I said.

It read:

Times of burglaries
1. 3:45 A.M.
2. 4:15 A.M.
3. 8:20 A.M.
4. 7:55 A.M.
5. 11:43 A.M.
6. 9:00 A.M.
7. 5:34 A.M.
8. 2:56 A.M.
9. 4:22 A.M.
10. 7:33 A.M.

"The chief might need this. But jot it down anyway." I said. Dylan jotted it down as quickly as possible.

Back at police headquarters, I said, " You may need this." holding the paper up.

"No, you'll need it. You're great detectives. You will be able to solve this in a snap." Chief Besmal stated.

"Maybe we should take the diamond ring to every jewelry store in town." I suggested.

"Okay." Chief Besmal replied. They took it to every jewelry store in town. Only one store said yes to seeing the diamond ring ever since they had started working at that specific jewelry store.

"I didn't see or hear his name but I saw a code on his shirt. The code was 113119 1012341." the man said.

"113119 1012341", Dylan repeated, "that stands for AMAS KAWDA!" They had 1 list of gangsters, with 9 names, ending with Amas Kawda! But the names were in code, part of which looked like this:

2152 1651692015, 101145 42114149147 AKA 2085 111181205 38151616518

"It says the names are Bob Pepito, Jane Dunning AKA The Karate Chopper, Joshua McCarthy, Bob, Scott Turner, James McGee, Parker Aber, Shooter Boudreaux, and Bill Taft. This is the gang of Amas Kawda!" I said excitedly after I translated the words.

"We will need a phone book. Let's go buy one." Dylan suggested.

They bought a phone book and then went back home.

"Why do we need a phone book now, Dylan?" Dylan explained why they needed a phone book then and I steadily agreed.

"To get the addresses of the bad guys!" I said.

And suddenly without notice a bomb flew into the house with a note. It read:

Stop your meddling around here or else! Ha! Ha! Haaaa!

Then, we continued our search for the addresses.

B.P.	8675309	478 Jefferson St.
J.D.	8673971	352 Easy St.
J.M.C.	8678113	1176 Fare St.
B.B.B.	8675432	567 Elm St.
S.T.	8671234	561 Maple St.
J.M.	8670123	465 Willow Lane
P.A.	8671802	657 Harper St.
S.B.	8671780	456 A Ave.
B.T.	8671592	785 15th St.
A.K.	8673653	896 Jamaame Dr.

Just then the phone rang. It was their dad. He asked about the case. They had a long discussion. Attached to the first note was a second note.

It said:

Hard heads will make the bread. The big boy day now. Sorry. Got everything.

To Harlan, Edward, and Madison.

"Let's count the 1, 8, 15, 21, 23, 31, 35, 36, 43, 48, 51, 59, 64, 66, 72, and 81st letters out." they suggested.

They did and it spelt H-A-M-E-R-B-O-Y-S-G-E-T-T-H-E-M. " Hamer Boys Get Them." Dylan said.

"That means we MUST be extra-cautious." I said angrily.

"I have a feeling." Dylan 'sang'.

"Were gonna get in big, bad trouble." I continued.

Just then they heard a ticking sound.

"THE BOMB! ITS ON 45 SECONDS!" I shouted loudly.

"To the bathroom!" Dylan screamed. 30 seconds! Lock! 15 seconds! Hide. 10,9,8,7,6,5,4,3,2,1,0, BOOOOOOOOOOOOOOOOM!

Out of the bathroom, Dylan said "Wheee-ewf. That was close." They were both shaky of the purpose bomb.

"We'd better call Dad and the police with Chief Besmal." Kyle said.

"With Roger, Mary, Kim, Bobby and Marty." Dylan added. They found another note sticking out of the wall.

It read:

Put in number code to get password of ARIAL ATTACK B.

1189112 SP 120201311 SP 2

"Easy." I said.

"Well where?" Dylan asked.

"Dylan, I've told you many times, Arial Attack is a series of buildings from A-Z. B is a letter of the alphabet, O.K.. It's in Washington."

In the car, they went through Vermont, New York, Pennsylvania, Ohio, Indiana, Illinois, Wisconsin, Minnesota, North Dakota, Montana, and into Washington. In Arial, Washington, there was a big building with a B on it. There was a pad on the door that looked like this:

```
1   2   3
4   5   6
7   8   9
SP  0   *
```

He punched in 1189112 SP 120201311 SP 2.

"Password accepted." the computer said. The door was still locked. The roof turned. Corners moved. The roof moved down. A part of the wall fell down.

The boys went inside.

....

A door slid open. There were Bob and all the rest of the gang.

"10 AGAINST 2!" Amas said. But just then their dad, Marty, Roger, Bobby, Mary, Kim, and Sammy Porterly, came through the door.

"Wrong, idiot, 10 against 9! Do you know how to count? Do you know your numbers?" Albert said.

"Ooooh, boohoo, were so scared. We don no our numbers." I did a karate kick on Amas. Dylan did a judo spin on Bill. Their dad went for Parker and got a double-punch on him. Marty jumped up and belly-slammed Jane. Roger karate chopped Scott. Bobby hit James 100 times. Mary tripped Bob. Kim kneed Bob 2, the second Bob. Sammy and I pushed Shooter down. Dylan kicked Joshua to the wall.

"From now on we stick together on this mystery." Marty said. After they left, all got up.

We registered into a hotel. Dylan and I were in room 2000. Marty and Mary were in room 2001. Albert and Sammy were in room 2002. Roger was in room 2003. Bobby was in room 2004. They went to their soccer practice.

While doing this, Dylan was leaning on the goal when he heard a loud rrr. Dylan and I stepped back. Suddenly the goals turned around. Then the soccer field tilted. They fell under it.

"I'm getting out a here." Marty said.

"Marty, the roof is already closed. We'll find a way out." I said.

After talking to Mary he said, "You probably couldn't fit, anyway!"

There were so many soccer balls. Marty had to count.

After Marty had said he had counted 113 balls and Mary counted 119, I said, "That's it! 113 in letters are AM and 119 in letter form is AS. Put AM and AS together and you get AMAS!" I said.

"Right. Thank goodness you counted those balls." Albert said.

"But I don't get the connection with soccer balls and Amas." Dylan said.

"Maybe he takes soccer practice, too." I said.

"I didn't know bad guys took soccer practice." Marty said half-listening.

"It's a possibility." Dylan said.

"Don't give up hope that he doesn't." Albert said. There was a doorway. They were going in.

Mary said, "Don't say I didn't warn you." "Yeah, what she said." said Kim.

"We'll be careful." Sammy Porterly said.

When they exited, I wrote a letter.

It read:

We don't have to stop meddling. We have got seven more people.

The Mysterious Mystery Stranger was me. All of them had nicknames. Dylan had Smart Stranger. Albert had Thinking Stranger. Roger had Basketball Stranger. Bobby had Boat Stranger. Mary had Sister Stranger. Kim had Friend Stranger. Marty had Mystery Stranger. Sammy Porterly had Attendant Stranger.

But when AMAS got the letter, he went RRRRRRRRRRRAAA, and said, "I hate those Hamer Boys. They're ruining our plans."

"Sure." I thought, "I'm ruining his plans for justice." They went back into the hotel. They had a good sleep.

They had breakfast, which was delectable pancakes with butter and syrup, biscuits, and a tall glass of cold milk.

They assumed that they were going back to detective work, and you can guess what: they walked out of the snow-white door into the convertible to start their most likely daily (until the mystery was solved, that is) detective labor.

Marty sighed.

....

When the nine started detective work, I thought," I'm ruining their plans again."

Chapter II
Ruined Plans

DYLAN

There they were, thinking what to do after the search. Kyle said, "Hey, there's a piece of paper on the roof!"

"Good thing I have two duplicates of spring-shoes in my backpack." Marty said. He took them out. The sign on the glass said ' Break in case of emergency. '

"Give us a couple." Kyle said. He broke all three-glass boxes. After putting them on, Kyle got the note. It was in Morse code. The boys knew Morse code. It read: ··--- ····· ·---- ··---· ----· ----· · ---- ---· ···· -· · ----· ····-· -· -· -

Kyle said," It's a lot of stuff to uncover, but lets do it." After doing this, it looked like this: 251521185 1915 4514.

"This is what I call a double-coded code." I said. After uncovering the 2nd stage, it looked like: You're so dead.

"Who is this from?" I asked.

"Probably Amas' letter." Kyle said.

"That means you have to be extra-extra careful." Roger said.

"Roger's right. No telling what you might run into." Albert said, "Wait, there was a piece of paper attached to it." noticing the torn staple.

He got a super-microscope for the smaller print in between the big print and read: Codes for buildings A.A.A-Z, A.7385 B.MINE C.8264 D.9736 E.8111 F.1725 G.1075 H.8271 I.7989 J.1811 K.6382 L.1587 M.2384 N.6799 O.1111 P.1999 Q.1463 R.2222 S.1234 T.5678 U.9012 V.3455 W.6789 X.0333 Y.4444 Z.5555.

"Jot this down." Albert commanded. He repeated the message. B.MINE, Hmmm. it's from AMAS, all right. They decided to take the note to police headquarters.

They did so and found out it was indeed from Amas. They decided to go back home. All of them went home. The next morning the two boys found their Aunt Denise in the kitchen making breakfast. It was 8:30.

Aunt Denise scolded, "Why are you so late getting up? You always get up at six. Your dad isn't even up, either. Do you have an explanation for that, too?"

"We all had a big day yesterday." Kyle answered.

"How big?" Aunt Denise asked worriedly. Dylan told her about their day while they ate.

"Oh." Marie, Marty's sister, said. She had just appeared from the den.

"But eat your breakfast. It's getting cold." Aunt Denise scolded.

"Marie, do you ever get the feeling that they're going to get up this late every day from now on?" Aunt Denise whispered in a light and soft voice.

"Ummm. We can hear every word that comes out of your mouth." Kyle said.

"Then let me challenge you. What did I say?"

Then Kyle said," Marie, do you ever get the feeling they're going to get up this early?" Marie whirled around as if she was going to answer the question.

"N" -- "I asked them to repeat what I said because they were being smart alecks." Aunt Denise said.

"Oh." Mrs. Hamer said. When the boys set off for detective work, they were actually ruining Amas' plans. His plans were is to make them so busy, he wanted them to sleep all day so he can get on with stealing more stores.

But the Hamer's wouldn't let him. Although they got up at 9, he wanted to start at 9:15.

"I should have planned it earlier." Amas mumbled under his breath. Not only that, but he got up at 8:30, and made fresh footprints. Meanwhile, the boys found the tracks and were following them. They were zigzag. It led to Amas' hideout. While Amas wasn't looking, they peered into the window. They knew it was Amas' hideout. My brother looked at the address and jotted it down.

It was 435 Long St.

"Now all we have to do is bring this home and show Dad when he awakens." Kyle whispered.

They went back home. They found Dad awake.

"Dad, we know where Amas' hideout is. It's 435 Long Street." Kyle said. Then they told him about their morning.

"Wow, you've accomplished a lot." Albert exclaimed.

"Time for lunch!" Mrs. Hardy said. The 5 ate lunch.

"But what you didn't accomplish is still a mystery." Mr. Hardy reminded them.

"We need to make a list of 'knowledge'." Kyle said. It said:

Knowledge	Want to Know
Who the gang is	How
Where Amas' hideout is	When
When millionaire is hiding	Solve Mystery

"There's probably more." I said.

"We'll have to add to it." Kyle replied. The boys hired a policeman on duty for the rest of the day. The next day the boys got up at regular time.

"Glad you're back to your normal *'routine'* today." Aunt Denise said, noticing the time they got up. They ate breakfast and set off for detective work.

Chapter III
Mad Amas

KYLE

Just then, unnoticeably, Amas ran for them and knocked them out. He put them in the woods. When they gained consciousness, they found themselves bound and gagged in the woods. They scooted sideways and untied their hands with each other's help. They untied their feet and took off their gags.

After getting up, Amas came running straight toward them! They dodged to the right. Amas turned around left and right, barely missing trees, running straight for them again!

This time they dodged left.

Straight ahead was Amas, grunting. "You've ruined my plans for the first time, probably ready to ruin them again!"

"Amas, Amas, Amas." Dylan said.

"We ruined your plans because you're a bad guy who needs to be in police headquarters." I said, "Were good guys."

"I've got a good computer in my brain. I filed then I got 321,598 suggestions to killing you." Amas said.

"1. Knock you off this mystery. 2. Kill you. 3. Lock you in a-- Amas continued but I interrupted-- " We don't need to know all 321,598 of them."

"But for now I'll do plan 1." Amas said, " Knock you off this mystery."

"You can't knock us off our mystery!" Dylan exclaimed.

"Right!," came a sound behind them. It was Marty. The boys gave a sigh of relief.

"You can't knock my friends off a mystery like that!" Marty snapped his fingers and continued, " I try to do it myself and they say" -- Marty said but I and Dylan said together, "Marty, we just like to solve mysteries and we like to help people."

"See what I mean?" Marty said.

"Yep, it's true." came another voice.

"He's right," said another voice. Marty gulped. From the darkness came Roger and Bobby.

"How'd you get here?" I asked then continued, "I know how Marty got here. I see his automobile."

"We drove up in the darkness so Amas wouldn't suspect anything." Roger said.

"Who knows how?" came 2 girl voices and a man's voice.

"And…we thought we should bring some other friends along." Bobby said. Appearing from the woods came Albert, Mary, and Kim.

"Game's up." Mr. Hamer said. But it was too late. 8 men from Amas' gang jumped behind them. They all woke up bound and gagged. There was nothing they could do. They were separated from each other. The only hope was if someone would come. Hours past. Suddenly a helicopter roared into sight. The eight waved to the men. The helicopter quietly sunk and came down to rescue them. The boys were untied and someone removed the gag.

"Boy, am I glad to see you." Marty said, expressing his thoughts. The other seven got up.

"I thought we were doomed for a second." I said.

"Kyle, Dylan, Mr. Hamer! Are you O.K.?" Sammy Porterly said.

"Yea, but what are you doing here?" Dylan asked.

"I'm his attendant, right. Well, you're on the TAA's blimp." Sammy said.

"What does TAA mean?" I asked curiously.

"The Attendant Association." Sammy answered. I just noticed that Sammy Porterly was Mr. Hardy's attendant. They had a long conversation. Meanwhile, in the woods, Amas looked back to check on the boys and was shocked.

"What the!" Amas screamed. Now they knew he was after the diamond ring. They were dropped off. They dropped the others off at their houses. Then they themselves got home.

"Chief John called for you." Mrs. Hamer said. I got on the phone and dialed.

"Chief, did you call for us?" I asked.

"Sure did. Did you find any clues?" The Chief asked.

Then Dylan started conversing, "One, the Arial Attack buildings have to do with this -- Dylan interrupted -- " Two, we know what he's after is the diamond ring, so put it somewhere where he cannot get it."

While they were conversing, a windowpane on the roof was removed. They said bye, but they both accidentally left the receiver on. Then a whole lot of commotion and noise came from the phone.

"We have got to help the chief!" I exclaimed. They ran to police headquarters. It was a mess.

"What happened here?" Dylan asked himself. Bars were bent, and people were knocked unconscious, all sorts of bad things. I called a doctor while Dylan kept a sharp eye out for any other vandalism.

When I arrived with the doctor, he said," Holy smoke!" He checked all of them then said, " No serious trouble though."

"Let's go to headquarters." Kyle said.

"We ARE at headquarters, you idiot." I said.

"No, I mean a Utica's headquarters. Utica is the nearest town." Kyle said. Just then Dylan noticed that Officer Richard was gone.

"To Utica!" I shouted. They drove straight to Utica. They reported what happened and put out a 28-state alarm for him. Actually it was from New York, Illinois, Pennsylvania, Ohio, Michigan, New Jersey, Virginia, Massachusetts, Indiana, Wisconsin, Maryland, Kentucky, Connecticut, West Virginia, Maine, New Hampshire, Rhode Island, Delaware, Vermont, Arkansas, Kansas, Iowa, Oklahoma, Colorado, Louisiana, Minnesota, Missouri, and a Texas state alarm. Back in Bayport, the people at headquarters were gaining consciousness.

"What happened?" one officer groaned.

"While he was talking on the phone -- pointing to the Chief -- Amas broke in and knocked everyone out. By the way, Officer Richard is gone and we put out a 28-state alarm for him." Dylan stated.

"What!" Chief John shouted, " He just d-d-d-disappeared." Then he almost fainted, "I also asked him to go on a job with me." Chief John stated.

"Tell us all about it." they said leaning in excitement.

"There was this man, Adas Kamta, who was bad," -- Chief John said but I interrupted -- " That's it! Adas Kamta is alias for Amas Kawda!" Chief John continued," We needed to get him. He has a gun."

"So we need something stronger than a gun." Dylan commented.

"Right. But what is stronger than a gun?" Chief John asked. They took turns guessing and another would decide...

"Metal, cement, wood, iron, knives, pocketknives, and baseball bats." But then I said,

" But what if we fight guns and guns?" I suggested.

" Sounds perfect!" the chief said. They went to the gun store.

" How may I help you?" the man said.

"We'd like" -- I paused to count – "8 guns, please. He handed them 8 BB guns and left. It was so long they even had a tracker, built-in to headquarters, and a GPS not built-in to headquarters. They followed it and then the red dot tracking Adal, and it was time for some action. They got out their guns and shot.

"By the way, he doesn't just need to go to jail, but die. He killed 5,000,192 people already." Chief John said. Then I said, "Then he's not Amas. He only killed a few.

Just then Dylan screamed," Tear gas bomb!" They rolled up the window and ducked quickly. But I shot a bullet out the window and it hit Adal in the chest. Adal fell to show a mechanism of working parts.

"No wonder he was so hard to defeat. Kamta was made out of metal." Chief John said. "Guys, guys, guys, always after me, eh?" Amas said. The police had already ducked. When he came closer the police took him by surprise. "Happy jailing!" the police said. The chief himself took out the handcuffs but he had already escaped.

"Don't say I didn't say that we would catch him this early in the part of the mystery." Dylan sighed. "I don't blame you, " Chief John said, "But back to the story." Even driving the Chief said, "He was in our way too much. He would drop by at lunchtime and wreck the place up." " Like literally mess the place up?" I asked. "Nearly every 3 days. When we'd get back, we'd have to clean it all up. It was time we stopped it. I asked him to come with me to stop him. I asked Chief Besmal" -- Chief John said but Dylan and I interrupted -- "Chief Besmal! The chief in Maine! We know him!" "Good. You can tell him the story of how we caught Adal Kamta and the watch is cancelled." Chief John said. "If we had enough time. We're out of it." Dylan said reading the newspaper, "Amas is ruling the top section of Maine." "What! Give me that!" I said grabbing the newspaper, "It really did happen, or it is happening." Chief Besmal's office, was wrecked the same way. When the sleuths found out, I said, "I wonder if the same thing happened here and there." "I don't know. Yet."

On the way home, they found three professors, Professor Andy, John, and Mark. They chatted for a while. When they rounded the corner, they didn't realize the professors had broken into a store or after talking because they were actually Bill, Shooter, and Parker in disguise as professors. I was reading the paper this time to see if there were any accidents or any other bad things around Bayport. Then I

20

read the headline: ROBBERY AT DRESSING STORE. "Dylan, come see this!" I said. "See what?" He said walking to me. Then he saw the headline. "Now I see." Then I said, "At Illinois Avenue there has been a robbery at the dressing store. Twenty-eight shirts, forty-six gowns, thirty-two jeans, eighteen pants, seventy-four pairs of socks, and twenty-three packs of underwear were stolen. The store is closed right now. It opens at 9:00." – Dylan interrupted -- "The owner's phone number is 564-5879. Fax: 758-2130. Others will be in phone book. Nobody knows any more, any less." "Did you notice the street sign?" I asked. "Nope." Dylan answered. "Well, we can find a store with a broken window on Illinois Avenue." I suggested. They did and looked at the street sign: Illinois Avenue. They found the store and went inside. The pants were up top, and 3 racks were empty. There was a merchandise hook used to grab beside them. They always brought their detective kit. They dusted for fingerprints and found some. "Chief John has a copy of the gang's fingerprints. I think." Dylan said hopefully. They drove to police headquarters. The boys went inside Chief John's office. I said, "Dylan thinks that you have fingerprints of Amas' gang." " Indeed we do." Chief John said. "Can we see them?" I asked. "Sure." the chief said, "No problem." They tried to find out who touched the merchandise hook, but couldn't.

When they got home, Aunt Denise was waiting for them. Then they sat on the couch and started watching the news. After about thirty minutes later Aunt Denise called, "Dinner's ready!" Just before they got into the kitchen, the news reporter reported, "Amas is now ruling the top section of Maine," which caught their attention. Immediately after dinner I exclaimed, "We better stop this before he rules us!" They got on their dirt bike motorcycles. Then they decided to bring their friends Marty, Albert, Bobby, Roger, Mary, Kim, and Sammy. They did so and set off for Maine. When they got to Maine, they saw a building about a couple thousand feet long. On the side of it of the building, I read: THIS BUILDING IS ARIAL ATTACK B. Then they remembered B. MINE on the paper. They punched in 113119 1012341. 'Password accepted." The computer said. A door slid open. Then there was another panel. It only had a . and a - on it. Then they typed in ·---- ·---- ·····-- ·---- ·---- ----· ·---- ----- ·---- ·---- ·--- ·····- ·---- and the computer said, "Password accepted." "Hope there's not a third. If there is, who knows what kind." Kim said. "Yea." Mary agreed. But there wasn't. Another door slid open. People were giving Amas anything. Soccer balls were rolling on the floor. "That's what soccer balls have to do with Amas. He uses them to torture the people." When Amas saw them, he said, "Get 'em!" They got them, took their vehicles and damaged them. They lay unconscious under lock and key. When they gained consciousness, they realized they were under lock and key. "Not so smart now." Amas said. Marty pulled out a pack of gum. "Hand me a stick of gum. I'm hungry." I lied. Marty handed him a stick of gum. Of course, he wasn't going to eat it. He was going to chew it, stick it on a stick, and grab the key with the gum. When he was trying to do it the first time, Marty said, "You said you were going to" -- then I interrupted -- "Shhh! Quiet!" He missed the key that time. The next few tries Marty ignored him. Finally, on the sixth try he got it. But his hand wouldn't fit through the bars. He had to solve that problem, and quick. But, his metal cutter! He could cut a few bars! He had to cut four bars before his hand could fit. He unlocked the jail cell door. They sneaked out of the building. "I'm NEVER going in THERE AGAIN." Kim said. "We might have to." I said. "But, hey, we survived." Dylan said being on my team, "But let's hit the road." "Actually I'm hungry." I said. "Now you're talkin' my spirit." Marty said. "But you're getting something small." Dylan said. "Oh, yea." I said. They walked to the nearest restaurant and ate. While there I said, "Where could our bikes be?" "I bet the police found them already." their dad said. They went back inside. They ate and called the police. They hailed a taxi for Manchester, Vermont. They went to police headquarters to find their bikes. They got their dirt bike motorcycles. When we got back home, I thrust the door of our bedroom. Well, what do you know, just like Vijay, a DOFT attendant, said, there was a package in our room. Ripping open the package we saw a disc. My brother inserted the disc into the computer. Their mission was to stop Amas' gang. And to be concealed. "In five seconds this disk will be reformatted into a regular CD." Q.T., the former leader of DOFT, said. Slowly counting to five, and as usual it was changed to Asian music. "Well whaddya think about the assignment?" I asked. "Simple." Dylan said. "Easier said than done." I said. "Let's see what else is in here." my brother said. Looking inside of the box, they found 2 M-4s, 2 rifles, 2 laser beams, 1 pair of handcuffs, and the diamond ring! Dylan started to pick it up. "They gave us the diamond ring to distract Amas not to hold and play with." I said, grabbing it out of his hand, "DOFT doesn't bring things that you don't need." "Humph." Dylan complained. "Let's go get Marty." I shouted over his complaining. I almost knocked him silly. "Why?" Dylan asked. I sighed and took out the handcuffs, and said, "You know why." "I shouldn't have asked." Dylan said. "Right." I said. In the car, Dylan asked, "How's Marty gonna help?" " Do me a favor. What is seven divided by three?" I asked. "Two with a remainder of one." Dylan answered. "You didn't have to ask me. You just answered your own question. Like, let me put it this way. If seven divided by three is two with a remainder of one, then we each get two weapons and I'll carry the handcuffs and we'll all get him." I said. "We'd better get the others." Dylan said. "No, if we do, we wouldn't have enough stuff and we'd have to go to the store, so let's just use what DOFT gave us." I disagreed. "Okay." he agreed. When they got inside Marty's house, I said, "What's in that closet?" I asked. "Figure it out yourself." Marty said, pointing to some number code and continued, "There's six more." The 1st one had 425141139205 on it. The 2nd one had 7211419 on it. The 3rd one had 51931165 812038 on it. The 4th one had 15208518 235116151419 on it. The 5th one had 31513519209212519/718212 1121915 615154 on it. The 6th one had 31513519209212519/718212 1121915 615154 2085 195315144 3121519520 on it. The 7th one had 51931165 8120 61517 1125125 1144 42512114 8113518 on it. They found out that the 1st one was dynamite, 2nd one was guns, 3rd one was other weapons, 4th one was escape hatch, 5th equipment for other reasons, 6th one was pizza and hamburgers (extra in freezer), and the 7th one was escape hatch for Kyle and Dylan Hamer. "Marty we need you to open the 1st, 2nd, 3rd, 4th, and 7th." I said. "Why?" Marty asked. "So we can defeat Amas." I said. "Well, I suppose I could just give you the codes. But only if you don't tell anyone." Marty said. "The only person we'll tell them to is our dad. They always come in handy for him, too, you know." Dylan said. "He's okay to tell, then." Marty said, giving them the codes.

They looked like this:

28, 57, 10, 39, 47, 02
42, 35, 39, 59, 27, 09
43, 36, 37, 07, 25, 04
25, 19, 12, 53, 28, 08
36, 59, 30, 47, 27, 51
36, 43, 28, 19, 56, 30
39, 45, 23, 10, 24, 57
(P.S. Go shortest way to number)

"Guys, I have to go." Marty said. After looking at it, I said, "Apparently it's a combination lock. Stop messin' around. Let's go!" With Dylan at the lock, I read, "1. 28, 57, 10, 39, 47…" and so on. I flipped my camouflage white board to a chalkboard, and said, "Here's the plan. We get guns, two sticks of dynamite, and a lighter -- " He was interrupted because the power went out. I said, "Don't worry. I know how to light a light bulb." I took 3 D-cells batteries, a light bulb, and 51 inches of wire. "You might have to help me." I said, "You can hold the batteries while I connect the wire to the negative part of the first battery and the other side of the wire connects to the side of the light bulb. I'll grab the tape." I said. After some quick addition, I said, "Three batteries make seven and a half volts." "Listen. This isn't science class." Dylan said. "But we need light if I'm gonna explain the plan." I said. Dylan held the batteries while I taped them. I also twisted the wire to the bottom of the battery. I connected and taped the other side to the light bulb and it lit! "Back to the plan. Part II. We go outside with the supplies and hide behind a bush. We throw a dynamite stick at a bush diagonal from us. It'll blow up and he'll look at it. We throw another stick at Amas. He'll blow up. The explosion and commotion will get the other eight. They don't have guns. We shoot at the bush across us. We shoot them, they die, and we win! We'd be done with the mission and all that's left is to solve the mystery!" I said. "Four questions. One. How are we going to solve the mystery? Two. Do you have a Plan A for that? Three. What if your Plan A is a failure?" Dylan asked.

"Stop jumping to conclusions." I said. Then the light bulb went out but Dylan had one in his head. "Maybe we can look up the diamond ring in the library." he said. "What does that have to do with this." I asked. "I don't know but you never know." he replied. And he was right. We went to the library. They looked in the 900s. Ancient diamond rings were from 913.27 to 913.79. The books were in the section 913.45 and 913.67. We checked out the books and I read, "The diamond ring was made by a man named Steven Smith. He finished it in 1957, died in 1971, and lost it. It was found 6 years later in 1977.

"Mark Sullivan was the owner of a diamond ring and treasured it. Mark died 15 years later in 1992. The ring was left in a treasure chest." "What's it say in the other one?" my brother asked. I flipped to the page and said, "Same thing." When we got home, I looked on the Internet. I typed in, "When was Amas Kawda born?" It said, "February 6, 1992". That's how he learned it! "That's it!" I said. "He would have learned it one way or the other." Dylan said after hearing the information. Just then I spotted a sheet of paper in the wall. I snatched the paper and read: 2515211212 14522518 4585120 135! After decoding the message I read: You'll never defeat me! They assumed that it was from Amas. Then I smelt something. Something like smoke. "Fire!" I yelled. Nobody else was home, good thing. Not cool. It wasn't easy, but with the help of our handy-dandy fire hose, we did it! We drove off into the central Bayport near the carnival.
"I think I see sparks." Dylan said.
"Can you stop using your imagination for one second?" I asked.
"I'm not using it!" he replied. Then I actually saw them myself. We went closer to the sparks. It was actually a broken and super-fast going carousel! *Not cool.* We had to stop it, but how? Then it struck me on the head. Just like a merry-go-round. You jump on it. Thank goodness that there was an empty horse.
"Follow me." I said. I leaped onto the empty horse and swung on the pole. I landed hands and knees on the metal floor. My brother shrugged and did the same. He landed the same way I did but crashed into the centerpiece. We got up.
"We need a plan." I said, "You got a rope?"
"No, but I got a belt." Dylan replied. "Okay. We both hold onto the belt while I hold onto the pole. You grab onto the control panel" -- I said but Dylan interrupted -- "There is no control panel. It's

automatic stop and start. But for a limited time." "Well then let's just wait." I said.

"Come on." my brother said.

"Why?" I said.

"Come on!" he blasted.

"Let me." I said as if I were reading his mind. We jumped off of the carousel. "Follow this cord with me." I said.

"No, you follow this cord with me." Dylan refused.

"Bossy pants." I mumbled under my breath. We followed the orange cord into a door. Inside there was a power generator. "Duh. What was I thinking? Cushions? What? Well, it wasn't a power generator. The power generator gave the carousel extra power. Help me pull the cord, I said. We pulled the cord and the carousel went back to normal speed. The kids got off.

"Whew. That was close." I said.

"You betcha." my brother said.

"We're going to Maine!" I exclaimed.

"Why?" Dylan asked.

"Because the whole thing has to do with him." I answered. When we got to Maine, we saw a new panel on the door. It looked like this:

1 2 3
4 5 6
7 8 9

It's problem changed, all right. The problem they had was 27 + _ x _ ÷ _ + _ x _ ÷ _ + _ =178. It took a long time to figure out that it was 27 + 56 x 5 ÷ 3 + 71 x 2 ÷ 2 + 24 = 178. Then the second panel had 31 + _ x _ ÷ _ + _ x _ ÷ _ + _ = 279. It took an hour to figure out that the solution was 31 + 57 x 6 ÷ 2 + 78 x 3 ÷ 2 + 15 = 279. Apparently Amas wasn't there. "Bingo." I thought, "Now we can investigate." One door read: TOP SECRET. KEEP OUT. Dylan found a code that said: Diamond ring code is ABDF5. They punched in ABDF5 and the door unlocked. Inside the door there was another problem code panel that read: 54 + _ x _ ÷ _ + _ x _ ÷ _ + _ = 624, by the way when u open this u will c a fake diamond ring. "Must be pretty lazy to do that." I said. "Maybe he didn't have enough room." Dylan concluded. "Shut up." I said, "He's got the whole door." Just then someone closed and locked the door. "Good thing I brought my pocket flashlight." Dylan said. "And Dylan did it again. Woohoo. Sheeshburgers." I said. They figured out that it was 45 + 15 x 3 ÷ 2 + 521 x 2 ÷ 2 + 6=624. The diamond ring 2 was in it. But there wasn't a niche of a way out. "Good thing I brought my handy-dandy blow torch." I said. "We don't need that. Let's just solve the problem." Dylan said. My brother thinks he's a mathematical expert and genius but he's not. "Okay." I said, "But this'll be hard. It's the 4th one we have been through." The problem was 34 + _ x _ ÷ _ + _ x _ ÷ _ + _ = 935. They soon found out that it was 34 + 56 x 5 ÷ 2 + 527 x 2 ÷ 2 + 183 = 935. They realized that the side door didn't open but they didn't notice that a secret trap door opened right under them! They crashed on top of each other under lock and key… again. Only two ways out but one was not possible. There was only one choice. "Blow torch?" I asked. "Blow torch." Dylan agreed. They cut a door out of the building. No, this isn't like Obi-Wan Kenobi fighting six droidekas trying to get to the door.

When they got home, Aunt Gertrude was waiting for them. It was almost midnight. "Why is it 12:00 at night when exactly you get home? It's not New Year's Eve, you know." she said. The next day, they went back to Amas's hideout. There was another problem that looked like this: 43 + _ x _ ÷ _ + _ x _ ÷ _ + _ = 1, 224. They soon found out by doing mathematics that it was 43 + 71 x 4 ÷ 2 + 711 x 2 ÷ 2 + 285 = 1,224. Apparently it was so early that Amas wasn't there yet.

"That's bingo two times in a row." I said.

"He could be hiding." Dylan said.

"You don't know that yet." I said. They sneaked from where they were to the door. They went back to where they were as I said, "Hey. A key." They found a lock. They put the key in the lock. There was a paper under it. It said: CODE TO SECOND PROBLEM PANEL IS 83045. They typed in 83045 and the first panel made a SHOOOP sound while it was sliding down. Another panel appeared. "Guess." I said. "83045." Dylan answered. A GZHZHZHZH sound was heard and the door slid open but another trap door went under them! They hung on to the trap door's door. Finally they squirmed out of it. They ran out of the door, exhausted. They got home about 9:30 p.m. and Aunt Gertrude sarcastically said, "Much better. How about some waffles?" "Sure." we said. We ate dinner. Afterwards I said, "What should we do now?"

"You're confused? I always thought you were the genius. But I don't know. I'm confused even more than you." Dylan answered.

"By the way, your father is out of town." Aunt Gertrude said. They sat there, thinking, but anything wouldn't plop out of their heads. After three more hours, I said, "I've got it! We can see what Amas is doing suspicious!"

"One problem." Dylan said, "How are we going to find him?"

"Easy. We know the address to his hideout. He's influential in Maine. So he's either at the hideout or the building." I said. "Nah." Dylan disagreed, noticing the clock, "He's probably is stealing a store. It is 12:30 p.m.. "

I turned to notice the clock. It was 12:30. "Maybe not." I said. "I'm calling it a day." Dylan said. I didn't fall asleep, but I sat there in bed thinking and thinking about what we would do. By 1:15 I was falling asleep. The next morning they got up at 9:15. We needed a new suggestion. We were thinking when we heard a slam from the door.

"Dad!" we shouted, putting aside the case.

"Hi. How was your trip?" I said.

"Good. I actually solved a mystery." Dad said.

"Wow. That fast?" I said.

"Yep." Dad said.

"We can't seem to figure out a suggestion for us to do on the mystery." I said. "Hmm." Dad hummed, "What about acting like thieves to get closer to Amas, and he may give you information."

"No. I'm not good at acting." Dylan disagreed. Dylan wasn't good at acting. Period. "Good point." Dad said.

The filled the details of the case to help him.

"Interesting." Dad said, "You can look up on-line for thieves and be them to get to their hideout for info. It's worth a try."

"No." Dylan disagreed.

"Let's at least try." I said, convincing my brother.

"Okay." he steadily agreed.

We went on-line to find 2 thieves. I was interested in Steven Flurry. Dylan was quite interested in Dave Brooksville. We were leaving when Aunt Gertrude asked, "Where are you going so early in the morning?"

"Uh, it's the Canadian Halloween." I lied.

"Yea, Aunt Gertrude." Dylan put in. Aunt Gertrude never looks at the calendar. She actually looked at the calendar and said, "The Canadians Halloween is on February 23, though."

"Wait a second. What was I thinking? Our friends are having a masquerade party today," I lied. She let us go, but no, we weren't going to a masquerade party. We were going to set off for Plan A. When we got to 435 Long Street, I said, "I suspected he would be at the hideout." There was security at the door. For our great disguising skills, we got inside easily. "I bet there's no more security anything." I said. But I spoke to soon. There was a security metal detector. When my brother got closer and it got clearer, my brother read, "THE DETECTIVE" DETECTOR. My brother elbowed me and whispered, "Uh-oh. You'd better read that." I read and said, " Oh, don't worry. I tripped the cord back there. " My brother looked back and saw a cord lying on the ground. So I saved us and thanks to my tripping skills, there wasn't beeping from "The Detective" detector. When they got in the main room, Amas said, "Hi. I'm Amas. I know you like to be called by your real name, but I give everyone a nickname. You see, everyone in here has a nickname. Well, I guess I'll just give you a nickname. Like Steve and Charlie." We sat down and listened, "Okay. We need to write this down." Amas said. And we wrote the plan. Amas noticed Dylan when his wig flew away while we were trying to escape in the car. Then he knew who I was. Me. Kyle. "What the heck!" Amas said, screeching to a halt. We turned back around to the hideout. They put them under lock and key… for the third time, but a way different kind. And the kind that has spikes that move in on you! We had to move quickly, really quickly. "Come on, birdbrain!" I said. I had to drag him half of the way there. We went through the Emergency Exit. Nope, it wasn't an emergency exit. Another jail. And I can't even describe it. And there's one thing I could do. Fall apart.

"Don't worry. The blowtorches? We can use them as flying equipment!" Dylan suggested.

We started flying as I said to Amas; "You can meet us at 531 Maple Drive." That was Marty's address. And we would be ready for him, or even *them*. We would bring all of our friends and fight. We busted out of there in no time. We zoomed to Roger's, Marty's, Kim's, Sammy's, and home to get Dad to plan a 'surprise' for Amas tomorrow.

The next day at Marty's house when Amas showed up, Dylan and I were standing right in the middle and we had our hands behind our back like we were all tied up. But so did Amas.

"Bring it on!" he said.

"Oh, yeah?" I said.

"Yeah." Amas said.

I signaled my friends to bounce out. They did and Amas said, "Bounced right back to you." using the same signal that we used and they bounced out, too.

"Battle?" Amas said.

"Battle." I said. We had learned new moves. And they didn't.

"We'll take care of it." I said.

"Then why did you get us?" Roger said.

"In case we need help." Dylan answered for me.

"Oh." Kim said. Amas spun on me on my left leg like a compass or a really fast going carousel making a circle 200 times. But apparently we just went on a carousel, so I guess he was tired of the spinning, because he wasn't doing the move that I'm doing, and I don't much care about that. I crashed him into the wall. "Ooooh. That's gotta hurt." Marty said.

"That's my boys," Albert said. Meanwhile, Dylan was doing the trick-trick. "Hold on to this." he said, pointing to a broken baby rocker. And he did. The 'audience' stared at Dylan in amazement. He flipped and kicked him on the head and he flipped himself about 50 times until finally he crashed headfirst into the ceiling and jumped off. Meanwhile, "Let's do addition." Dylan said as if he were stupid, "10 kicks + 30 punches + 50 hits + 1 poke = 1 kill." Trying it, it worked. "So he died. So? We have got 9 left. But we got ONE kill and we probably will need NINE more to get TEN!" I thought but I could have screamed the same exact words to Dylan in his ear. The rest were knocked out cold. "That'll keep 'em busy… if you know what I mean." I said. "Yes, we know what you mean." Dylan said. We walked out of the door. Ten minutes later they gained consciousness and tried to wake up Scott. "Why are you trying to kill him again when he's already *dead*?" Amas said. "What?" Amas' partners said together, not including Scott. "Dylan Hamer killed him!" Amas shouted in their ears. They almost fainted. "We would have saw it, right?" Bob said. "You were to attracted to Kyle's *show*!" Amas screamed at Bob, "So do you think so! No!" Meanwhile, at home, we were searching in our minds for a lead to follow up. Five minutes later I had it, "That's it! We haven't gone looking for the missing millionaire!"

"That's right!" Dylan agreed. They should have ran into the door instead of... Aunt Denise. "Where are you going?" she asked. "Uh..." I said. But before she could say that we didn't answer her question, we zoomed out the door into the kitchen. We got all of our snacks. We got onto our motorcycles. Out of New York, into Pennsylvania, Virginia, North Carolina, South Carolina, Georgia, Florida, rented a boat across the Gulf of Mexico, into Cuba, out of Cuba, into the Caribbean Sea. Drifting across the Niagara Falls, we stopped abruptly at a two-way fork. "Straight or left?" Dylan asked.

"I choose left." I said.

"And I choose straight!" Dylan said. "Well there's 2 of us and only 1 boat, so we have to decide on something!" I said in a rude tone of voice but I actually meant to stay calm and be nice about it but I accidentally started an argument. Straight! Left! Straight! Left! ... The argument continued on and on. Then I accidentally turned the boat left. Then when the boat was about to hit something, Dylan said, "Watch out! Drive! Don't be a reckless driver!" After that I noticed what was going on and I twisted around and steered the boat. Then, just ahead was a great white shark! Luckily we had some harpoons and fishing rods in the boat. *Nice. The Accessory Boat Association here.* We threw them at him, and he scrammed. "That's the first time we have done an activity defeating a shark in years." Dylan commented, trying to act like he was about 67. "I know." I replied casually as I usually do. Two hours later I noticed where we were. "We're in the Caribbean Sea." I said. Fifteen minutes later we were exploring the coves. But we were tied up and put in a prison although we didn't do anything... except for snooping and trespassing. Well, I guess we deserved it anyway...

Chapter IV
New Plans

DYLAN

Five minutes after we got up, I asked,
"Do we have any blow torches?"
"None." I said.
"Harpoons?" Kyle asked.
"Nada." I said.
"Fishing rods?" Kyle asked.
"Zero." I said.
"Metal cutters?" Kyle asked.
"Zilch." I said.
"Anything?" Kyle asked.
"I cannot assist you. And stop asking so many questions, okay?" I said. I tried kicking it open. But Kyle pushed me away. "You probably can't do it either." I said. But when I opened my eyes he had the door open waiting for me. "The first thing you've gotta try is opening the door." Kyle said, "And sometimes you can be so dumb."

I rolled my eyes and said, "It's not obvious for someone to leave the jail door unlocked if someone is prisoner there. It's like giving your dog 8 chocolate bars. Do you expect that?" "Well, no" -- Kyle said but I interrupted -- "See, it's unexpected." "This will be a long day." Kyle grumbled.

"U-huh." I said sarcastically as if I had heard him. There were about 5,000 other jails, but none of them had a missing millionaire in them. Meanwhile, Kyle was counting the cells, "1856, 1857, 1858..." "I'll estimate 5,000,000 because you'll never count all of them." I said.

"Shhhhh." Kyle said. After that he started counting again, "1872, 1873, 1874..." One hour later I looked at my watch. 4:24! It had been 9 hours and 39 minutes! He showed Kyle a signal showing that it had been 9 hours and 39 minutes. They left and got home at 12:14 p.m.. They went to bed as soon as they got home. They woke up at regular routine, but they were still tired. And it was the regular-routine-routine-just-so-Aunt-Denise-would-be-happy kind of tired.

"Waffles?" Aunt Denise asked, "And why do you look so tired?" "Wellllll, " -- Kyle stretched out for me to finish -- "we got home at 12:14 p.m. and decided to wake up at our normal routine so you would be happy. We just wasted 2 hours." "Well then, go! My limit is two hours and thirty minutes!" Aunt Denise said like she'd gone through all of this trouble to say it. Two hours later in the same day, they woke up at 8:30 a.m. "Now waffles?" Aunt Denise said politely. "Yea!" Kyle said, almost screaming, rushing to the table, "I haven't had dinner and almost missed breakfast!" "Greedy." I mumbled to myself. There were pancakes for breakfast. Kyle was so hungry that he ate eight pancakes. "Pig." I mumbled so low that Kyle couldn't hear, "My brother is a big, fat pig." I said that because I only ate four. After that we sprinted out of the door. We drove down the road and I saw a moving Ferris Wheel full of kids and broken controls. *Broken controls!* I grabbed the steering wheel and spun it left. "Hey! What side are you on?" Kyle said. "I'm on the kids side!" I said, pointing to the Ferris Wheel, "We need to jam something in the thing that holds the switch! Like a fat stick!" grabbing a fat stick, but it wasn't too fat but it would have to do. *Have to.* We ran to the controls of the Ferris Wheel and put the stick in the thing that holds the switch. We adjusted the stick to the switch and pulled it really carefully. Finally the kids got off. All of the frightened and worried parents cried with joy. We ran down to the street for protection of thank you.

"I'm getting the picture. Amas capturing Adam is only a start to a much bigger plot to take over the world!"

"Notice everyone's plot is to take over or destroy the world." Kyle said.

"Yeah." I said, then continued, "Anyway, Amas is most likely planning to capture more millionaires and get more money. Then he'll gain so much money, he'll buy out the entire country, make everyone pay 20 times their regular taxes, and make a profit to seize the Earth, like… like… real estate!"

"That sounds evil all right." Dylan said, and we worriedly headed home.

When they got home, they opened the door and no one was home. "There's always someone here." I said.

That's when Kyle's 'sixth sense' started tingling. "There's something suspicious around here," he said. "How come I don't have that? Hello? Listen to me, why don't I have that…" my complaining went on and on. Two minutes later Kyle screamed, "SHUT UP! Can't you see I'm concentrating on something?" "Well," I sounded confused, "I guess so." Kyle hunted for clues and found a message. It said: We are in -- the message was never finished. "Weird" said Kyle. "I think that means someone in the family found somebody in the gang and started jotting down a note but got captured. Or maybe even all of them, Duhhh!" I said. "But you said ' or maybe even'." Kyle said, "And that means it could but you don't know the exact answer either." "Okay. Let me reform that sentence to 'they captured all of the rest'." I said. "Well, guess what, heads, I win, tails, you lose." Kyle said. It sounded confusing to me for a minute, but scanned his words and found out what I was going to say. "You sound like a Penny Pincher on Toon" -- Kyle interrupted -- "Blah, blah, blah, blah, blah." "Town." I finished. They stood there for a second then blasted off to find the others. They looked everywhere from high and to low, and from side to side. "There's only one place left." Kyle said, "The -- he paused -- attic." As he started walking toward the garage, then stopped and said to himself, "We need a flashlight." When Kyle started walking toward the garage, I said, "Wait! No!" Kyle turned around as I added, "I'll just do it myself." "You're hiding something." Kyle said. "No, I'm not," I said. "I don't believe you," Kyle said, now racing to the garage. "Darn it. I guess I just made it worse." I said where Kyle couldn't hear as I was tagging along and racing to stop him. Kyle was halfway up the steps when I got to him. Emergency steps were on the side, but this wasn't an emergency. I only had to find a way to beat Kyle up those steps! Oh, well. I guess I'll just have to go with the emergency steps. But there was one problem. The emergency steps went all kinds of ways. But, Dad gave the diagram, to Kyle. Thank goodness the ladder was long. I caught up with him and quietly snatched the diagram from his pocket and opened it. The diagram was easy, so I pretty much got up the stairs before you could say 'antidisestablishmentarianism'. Thank goodness Dad had explained that diagram good, because about two seconds later, Kyle stomped on the wooden floor of the attic. I blocked the way to my 'hidden things or junk'. Junk is what Kyle would say. But as they say, 'one person's trash is another person's treasure'. "Well, if you say you aren't hiding something, why are you acting like you are hiding something?" "Well… ummm…" -- I said but Kyle interrupted -- "Ha! You are hiding something. I told you! Told you, told you, told you!"

"Shut up!" I shouted. Then we heard 'mmm mmms' from a distance away. Kyle stood there like he didn't hear it or he's out of his mind. "Come on!" I shouted angrily. "Where?" Kyle asked. "To find our parents and friends!" I shouted. Kyle and I walked a few feet and Kyle said, "So anything you wanted to hide from me, you keep in the attic." I sighed. Kyle got me. He discovered that I kept my 'junk' in the attic. Kyle noticed my sadness and said, "Well, maybe I was a little harsh on you. But brother detectives have to share a few secrets sooner or later." "Well, I guess so." I steadily agreed. Still, I wasn't 100% happy, but at least I was 25% happy. But I was still 75% depressed. If he'd said that three more times in three different forms, I would be 100% happy. My mind started to wonder, "No, I'm just kiddin' with you. An apology would be nice. But saying 'Hello, you have something else to say' and Kyle saying, 'What?' and then me sayin', 'An apology would be nice' would be disrespectful. Okay, that's getting complicated. Just as I was about to pop my thought bubble, I heard a faint noise from Kyle saying, "Dylan!" I got my self in shape as quickly as possible and Kyle said, "Wow, you must've been sunk into that bubble like toilet paper clogged into a toilet. It been fifteen minutes" -- Kyle said but I had to interrupt -- "Fifteen minutes! That long?" " What were you thinking about anyway?" Kyle said. "Nothing." I said and went along. "I popped your dream bubble with nothin' in it?!" Kyle asked quizzically. "Yes." I answered. "And it took fifteen minutes?" Kyle asked. "Yes." I answered with the same answer. He though I had gone crazy! After a few moments Kyle thought about it, he said, "Alright." I assumed he said that so he wouldn't have to be rude again. Our parents were shoved into the P-supplies and our friends were clogged in the F-supplies. We untied everyone. They were grateful. "How thoughtful of Amas to hid them under the letters." Kyle stated. Kyle was thinking about how they had read on the internet that Amas had almost no education because he was a kindergarten drop-out. That reminded Kyle that maybe he should check his e-mail.

KYLE

I went to our room. We had gotten one e-mail. It was from DOFT (Detective Organization For Teenagers). It read:

Dylan and Kyle,
I can see how you are having trouble killing Amas. So we are sending you two assistants, Walter Gibbins, and Peter Bradey. If you have any questions, don't be afraid to ask.

Your DOFT member,
Vijay.

I went to the computer and typed a short return e-mail.

Vijay,
    Why two?

Kyle and Dylan.

Vijay responded

Kyle and Dylan,
If you split up, you'll both have one.

Your DOFT member,
Vijay.

I went back to the attic to meet Dylan.
"We're getting on the computer." he said. "You should have came down with me. I was on the computer a minute ago."
"Oh? Is that so?" Aunt Denise commented, "What were you doing while Dylan was here?"
"Typing a letter." I confessed.
"To whom?" Aunt Denise questioned him.
"Marty." I lied.
"Oh. Sorry I asked." Aunt Denise responded.
"Let's go!" Dylan said. We all ran to the computer.

DYLAN

Roger directed, "Go to the Internet." I typed Google .com, and I turned around and said,

"Okay, Roger, I'm to where I *can* handle it, you know." I clicked 'Criminal Info'. There was a bar that read: CRIMINAL YOU WOULD LIKE TO WEB. I typed in 'Amas' and pressed 'Enter'. It came to a full page about Amas!

"Good thing Dad has good IAS." Kyle said. (IAS means Internet Access Service)

Then I read, not listening to Kyle, "Amas was born on February 6, 1992. His parents died 3 years later on June 21, 1995. His mother's last words were, "Go to Aunt Sally's" -- Then she was cut off. Amas took a taxi cab to Aunt Sally's house. Telling the taxi man that his parents died, the taxi man let him go without paying for the ride. Aunt Sally was poor, and that was a problem. "Why was she so poor?" you may ask. She bungled every job interview, so she did not have a job. When Aunt Sally would always say, "But I am poor." She scarcely knew her math and science so she just didn't use them. The job interviewers would always say one of these three, "No can do, right?" And she would have to agree. Or, "We just can't take you." Or even, "I think this job is too hard for you.' Which was her cue that she had failed. Amas thought that the only possibility was to be a criminal and steal. Now, he is rich, like everybody assumes, Amas is still stealing from stores around the world."

"Well, that answers the 'why' on our KWL (knowledge) chart." Kyle said.

K	W
Who	How
Where	When
Where millionaire is	Solve mystery
Why	Kill Amas

"That 'why' is over with now." I said.

"At last." Kyle said, "We finally got 'why' and it only took a year!"

"Hush.. Kyle, it's only been two weeks." I said.

38

"It clears up 'when', too." Roger affixed, changing the focus, "1992 and 1995 from his birth date and parents' death."

"Right." I agreed.

K	W
Who	How
Where	When
Where millionaire is	Solve mystery
Why	Kill Amas

Just then there was a knock on the door. It was Peter Bradey and Walter Gibbins.

"Greetings." Bradey said, almost like an English alien.

"Hello." we said.

"What is this?" Gibbins asked.

"Internet research on Amas Kawda to help with 'when' and 'why'. Actually, here's a KWL chart." I lent him the KWL chart.

"Wow, you have even discovered where Amas's hideout is." Bradey complimented.

"Thanks." I said, nudging Kyle's arm.

"Yeah... Thanks." I glanced at Marty. He was eyeing his watch. I looked at the clock and sighed. 12:00. Lunchtime.

Then Kyle whispered, "I didn't wanna say with you."

"Yeah. Okay. Drop that. It's lunchtime, and, of course, Marty's wondering when we're gonna eat." I whispered. Then Kyle looked at Marty for a second, as I did.

"Splendid." he said sarcastically.

But then our savior, Aunt Denise, called, " Lunch is ready!" And, of course, like he always does at our house, rushed downstairs to the kitchen and dining room.

"There's ham or cheeseburgers today." Aunt Denise said, revealing the menu, "With a side of french fries. And milk or water." I was surprised that Aunt Denise did not ask about our guests. Marty disintegrated about three plates in a minute. I would say that is the best record I have ever seen.

Five minutes later, we were back on track. Well, not all the way. Because Kyle's radio was booming as loud as it could. Of course, it was on hard rock, Kyle's favorite.

Then I passed by, I pressed STOP on the radio. Kyle froze in his tracks for a second to press PLAY on the stereo. So I turned around, took the CD out, put it in its CD case, and put it on the highest space on the rack. Of course, he couldn't reach it. Oh, yeah, I forgot to mention, I was taller than Kyle.

"Whatever." he said.

"Now, where were we?" I asked.

"He just gave you back your KWL chart." Kim answered.

"What we need to do" Gibbins said, pausing, "is to find evidence and prove how Amas does it."

"Proof." I mumbled.

"Proof." I said.

"Proof!" I screamed, "Kyle, we forgot proof!"

I didn't notice but I was walking around in circles the whole time! I snatched the KWL chart and put 'proof' on the W side.

This is what it looks like now.

K	W
Who	How
Where	Solve mystery
Where millionaire is	Kill Amas
Why - Proof (of all except who)	When

"Well, if we're gonna find out how and prove it, the only way to do it is go to his hideout!" I said, excitedly.

"Which one?" Kyle asked.

"Which one?!" Marty asked quizzically, screaming. He jumped up.

"What do you mean, which one?" Marty asked, calming himself down from the confusion.

"We forgot to tell you that we found one on 435 Long Street, one in Maine, and one in Arial Attack B." I answered.

"Oh." Marty said.

"Okay, which one do we go to?"

"The one in Maine."

Once we reached Maine, I noticed something.

"Drive alongside the building." I said loudly.

"What?" Dad asked.

"One sec. Do not do anything." It was Marty.

He was singing over and over and over again, "This land is your land, this land is my land, from California, to the New York islands. From the redwood forest, to the Gulf Stream waters, this land was made for yooou and meeeeeeeeeeeeeeeee!" So I kicked him. But all he did was keep on singing.

I tossed him a Tek-mate (a device that allows you to send messages back and forth to each other) and he caught it. I gave him a thumbs-up sign.

I gave him a text message saying:

1. Drive alongside the building. 2. Shut up!

He turned around and drove beside the building, as I said. Not long before the building was ending, I saw a sign saying: Madawaska City Limits.

"Oh, no! Amas is starting to take over Presque Island!" I said. Marty had finally stopped singing, so I could talk to Dad.

When the building was ended I said, "Drive farther." I said that because I heard a faint sound of swords clinging.

"Holy macaroni!" I heard Marty say.

"What?" I asked.

"Look behind you." Marty sung.

I did so and after glancing at it, I said, "Oh my gosh. War!!!!" I screamed, "Over Amas and his friends versus Houlton citizens!"

Dad stopped the car. It screeched.

"Where?" everybody asked at once.

"There." Marty answered for me. We got out of the car and I whispered the plan. We walked up with our friends straight behind us.

"Oh, it's you. And I am glad there's only two." Amas said.

"Oh, really?" I said.

"Four." I corrected him.

"Six." He corrected me back.

"Eight." I said.

"Ten." He corrected me for the last time.

"Ten." I repeated, "Kyle, me, Gibbins, Bradey, Dad, Marty, Roger, Bobby, Mary, and Kim."

I checked them with all of my fingers.

"But we did not bring any weapons." Bobby pointed out. Marty was whistling loudly, leaning on the car.

"What are you hiding?" I asked, squinting my eyes.

"Nothing." Marty said. I climbed into the car.

Next thing I knew, I was tossing and throwing swords and guns, all kinds of weapons.

"That's what I was hiding." Marty sighed.

"I don't care about that right now – for that matter... I'll never care. Let's get into the game!" I said.

We tore over to help the Houlton citizens. The group split into two. One group was Kyle, Kim, Marty, Dad, and Bobby. Our group was Mary, Gibbins, Bradey, Roger, and I.

Many others were fighting Amas, but Kyle still thought it would be impossible to do it by themselves. Although they had to squeeze in, it was worth it. All he wanted to do was help the Houlton citizens.

The group did not follow him, however, because they would take him from different directions. The bad thing was that Amas had two swords.

Meanwhile, our group was fighting and fighting, and we had a good thing. It was that Chief Besmal had secretly switched sides! As soon as Amas found out, he pushed everyone aside, and stomped over to him. "Why did you change to the other side?" Amas asked.

Kyle spotted some bottles. "People littering is coming in handy today." He threw all of them at Amas.

"I'll get glass-busted." Amas realized, "I'll get glass-busted."

So he ran and shouted, "I'll get you next time!" Madawaska and Presque Island citizens ran after him. All except Chief Besmal.

"Hang around Bayport and you'll be alright." I invited him.

"Sure." Chief Besmal replied as if he knew what I was saying. It was the same back in Bayport. Detectives were still working on the mystery.

The next day was Independence Day. It was raining the day before yesterday, so it was still damp when we went to Roger's party at 1:00.

It would end at 5:00.

After three hours, I found a letter.

"Dylan, come look at this!" Kyle said, "And bring Roger."

Dylan had a cynical stance about this, for he was partying with his friends. He came over anyway, evidently that it was very important. And by my look he knew it.

So he rushed over.

42

First, I asked Roger if he had seen the letter.

He said, "No. In fact, I haven't."

"Then for crying out loud, what is it?" Dylan shouted quietly.

"Shut up!" I said angrily as I tore open the letter.

It read:

"Meet on top of Mt. Everest. 12:00-2:00. Using helicopter #428. Amas."

"Mt. Everest! That's... -- Dylan freaked out, looking in a book -- "29,035 feet! How are we gonna get there?! They'll spot" – I interrupted -- "Calm down. Dad and I will plan a charter flight to China and India with Chris Tucker."

"Pheeewwhh!" Dylan was relieved, "WAIT. I wanna do it." I knew he would get back to his senses.

But I said anyway, "Babies *can't* plan a charter flight. Ha ha ha. Roger started laughing as Kim joined in.

"What's this all about?" she questioned.

"We found a letter on the ground and picked it up, tore it open, read it, Mt. Everest deal, Dylan freaks out, told him we would plan a charter flight, Dylan freaked out again 'cause he wanted to. And that's the summary." I explained.

"Oh, no you won't. Last time you went to Japan instead of Greenland." Kim shot.

"And you think I'll make the same mistake?" Dylan retorted, "I'll get us to -- I interrupted – "Antarctica! Ha!"

"Rrrrrrrrrrrr!" Dylan sneered and left the party, took the convertible, and drove away. "Oh no!"

I said, "He must be heading for the airport!"

"Keys?" I asked.

"Keys." Roger said.

I took the keys, ran, and everyone ran after me. I put the keys in the ignition as Roger and Kim scrambled in. I drove in pursuit of Dylan until I found a detour. I drove through it and ended up at the airport before Dylan. I drove for the airport. As soon as I got there the convertible was parking.

"Come on. We have got to get there. And try not to attract attention." I said hurriedly.

"The sooner, the better." Roger said. We won and planned it before he did. The plane was scheduled to depart the next day. We, as in Kyle and I, got home and laid on the couch.

No sooner than that, we were asleep. The next morning, everyone was having a feast. After breakfast, we glanced at the KWL chart to see what we were going to try to conquer that day.

It was decided that we would prove where the millionaire was.

"But how?" Kyle asked.

"Well..." I started.

"Well, what?" Kyle asked.

"I'm thinking, I'm thinking. Well, the only thing I can think of is bringing the others personally and find him." I said, "But that would be stupid."

I sighed.

"Dylan, that was the BEST brilliance you've ever had!" Kyle cheered me up.

"Really?" I sobbed. Kyle had never said that to me before!

"But the only problem is that the Sleuth can only hold three people." Kyle said.

"Tony has a boat, Bobby's dad just bought him a boat, and Bradey has a single-rider boat for cruising." I said.

"O.K." Kyle said.

So we put our plan into action. We took separate cars to encounter the others. Dad came into the car with me. We would gather our assigned society. I was to get Bobby, Marty, Mary, and Kim, since they were close to each other.

Kyle was to round up Roger, Gibbins, Bradey, and Sammy, which was bad for him, because they were far apart. So, to help him, I told him that I would get as much as I could in one hour.

I started off like a race, but slowed down when I got to the major roads. It was 11:15, and it was packed!

"Where do you think all these people are going?" I asked to Dylan through the window, "They can't be going to work. Nor lunch."

"I sure don't know." Kyle answered, "I can't discover it right from the ground."

The green light interrupted our conversation. We had to get our friends. Fast! The maximum speed limit was 50 M.P.H., but because of traffic, either way would've been 30 M.P.H. anyway.

Then I heard Kyle's racket through the portable two-way radio that we just bought.

"Kyle, I can hear you." I said.

"What? How? Huh?" Kyle was confused.

I didn't expect him to say that.

"Well... apparently... uh... I guess...maybe..." I started rapidly.

"Well... apparently... uh... I guess...maybe..." Kyle paused, "What?"

"I guess you apparently flicked the microphone and the hearing system carried away in your racket and I started to hear you." I said.

"Oh." Kyle said back to me.

By that time I was at Roger's house. 'Time to nab my first customer.' I thought. I parked our car in the driveway of Roger's house. "I'll get him myself." I said. I walked up to the door and rang the doorbell. Roger's mom opened the door.

"Yes?" she asked.

"May I speak to Roger?" I asked.

"Sure." Roger's mom walked off as Roger substituted her absence.

"Roger, this is important." I started, "We need to 'set up' a camp-out to hunt down the missing millionaire. And we need all of the help we can get. So we decided to get you and our friends. You in?"

"Well, I'm kinda busy right now, so I'm afraid I can't come." Roger answered. "Well then, just meet us at Central Park at 12:15 to have lunch." I solved the problem.

"Okay." Roger started silently closing the door as if he needed to hurry if he were to be there by 12:15. I walked rapidly back to the car, as if I needed to go, too.

"Where's Roger?" Dad asked when I had hopped into the car.

"He's busy -- Dad had a frown on his face so I paused -- "but he'll meet us at the park."

I was on Libby Avenue where Bobby lives. I pulled into the driveway.

"Short drive." Dad said so slowly that I almost couldn't understand him. As I walked up to the door, I glanced around at things. It was so... different. But I tried to keep myself focused. There was no doorbell, so I had to knock.

Bobby opened the door and said, "Hi, Dylan. What's up?" I explained to him the way I explained it to Roger.

"Okay." he said afterwards. He jumped to the back seat of the car with the boat fitting into the trunk. "So, what's this campout thing for?" Bobby looked at me suspiciously.

"To hunt down Adam Aksaw." I said.

"What kind of name is 'Aksaw'?" Bobby questioned.

"Just a name, I guess. Last names are weird." I said as Dad chuckled.

I noticed it and shook a finger at him.

"It's just – just not all names are weird. So I thought it was funny of you to say that." Dad confessed quietly.

After two more roads, I was stopped at Gibbins and Bradey's house. I parked in front and got out of the car. It actually turned out that nobody was home. We drove off again as I checked my watch. 12:00!

Fifteen more minutes until I had to meet Kyle in Central Park!

"I better radio Kyle that I'll be there at 12:30, not 12:15." I agreed.

"Agreed." Dad said half-listening, concentrating fully on where he was going. Ignoring the way he said it, I picked up the microphone and flicked it to ON.

"Dylan to Kyle. Come in, please. Over." I said.

"Kyle to Dylan. Hear you loud and clear. Over." Kyle said.

"May be late. Extend time to 12:30. Over." I said.

"I can see why. Every house I've gone to, no one's there! Except for Roger, who told me you saw him." Kyle said.

"Oops." I checked my map and society, "Picked up more of yours than mine. Don't go to Gibbins and Bradey's. I'm there. Over." I said.

"O.K. Will pass up." Kyle said. I finally switched the microphone to the OFF button and put it back in its charger.

I was on 25th street on my way to Iola's house. I was about to call Kyle when he called me by surprise.

"Picking up Sammy. Do not pick up." he said. "Must have learned how to talk radio version." I said, impressed of the short time he had learned the way to talk on the radio like the way I did.

It kind of messed up my plans, so I had to think that over. As soon as Kim knew Mary and Kyle were coming, she sprinted so fast to the truck, I could not see her do it.

The trip was only five minutes, so we didn't have to hear her anticipation for very long. I got to Sammy's in ten minutes, and Central Park was nearby.

Dad insisted he'd do this one, and did it good, because he was in the car in a minute. We got to the park in time, and Kyle was waiting at a bench.

"What took you so long?" he asked.

"To pick up all of these." I said. Kyle stared in amazement as everyone piled out.

"Geez. How did you manage to pick up all of them?" Kyle asked.

"I guess you could say it was a miracle." I shrugged.

"Who has the lunch?" I asked Dad and Kyle.

"I do." Kyle answered. He left for the car, but stopped halfway.

"Where are Gibbins and Bradey?" he asked. "We should discuss that in private." I said in sign language, "It has something to do with DOFT."

"Right." Kyle said. We strolled farther away, but after that, whispered,

"They were at DOFT. Said they would meet here." Then the discussing the matter deeply came in.

Meanwhile, a car pulled up and they got out.

"You should tell him they're here, Mr. Hamer." Kim said, "Not us." Everyone else nodded. As he was leaving, another car pulled up behind Gibbins and Bradey's. Bobby recognized it as Roger's.

"Better tell 'em that, too." Marty said with a cowboy accent.

When he got over there he said, "Roger, Gibbins, and Bradey are here."

"Oh." I said.

We walked back and found everyone eating lunch. We ate as fast as we could, but they still beat us. We drove to Vermont. They walked a quarter-mile to their boathouses.

We set out for the Gulf of Maine.

Chapter V
Robots!

KYLE

"We should be at the Gulf of Maine, going to the Atlantic Ocean, past the Bahamas and West Indies, between Cuba and the Leeward Islands, then in the Caribbean Sea, take a sharp right before where we got in, then another sharp right and we should be at a docked cove. That will be the one!" I directed.

"Sounds complicated." Dylan said, still in radio talk.

"Knock it off." I said.

Although I wanted to say 'Shut up', I didn't want to be rude. I focused my attention to the boat trip. Then and there, was a gray image in the water.

"Sh-sh-sh-shark!" I shouted as soon as I recognized the grayish image.

"Good thing I brought the emergency boat ride A-Z supplies." Dylan said. Then I was relieved. Why didn't I think of that? Oh, well, at least Dylan remembered.

He'd grabbed the 19th bag and was looking through it. "Sh." he mumbled, "Sha. Shar. Shark!"

As he pulled out a Ziploc bag, I hollered in Dylan's ear, "Hurry up!" I grabbed the bag and dumped everything out.

I dug through the pile of 'shark' supplies.

After looking, I said question fully, "There's nothing useful in here."

But I pulled a pistol from my pocket, shot the shark, and it went down. The others stared in amazement.

"That's the better-than-the-emergency-boat-ride-A-Z-supplies-and-it-is-called-Kyle's-pocket-supplies." I said in his face, "And what did you put in the other bags?"

"Regular stuff." Dylan answered.

"Regular! Regular!! REGULAR!!!" I exploded, "That stuff wasn't useful to kill a shark at all!!!!"

My voice got louder as I talked.

"I didn't know what to put in there." Dylan sputtered.

"You're a brother+dad detective! Detective! Detective! Detective! Even more, brother detective! If you can't figure out something alone, you can ask me or Dad, birdbrain!" I erupted, "And next time, let me do that." I had calmed myself down a little.

By then they were paddling through the Atlantic Ocean. For the rest of the trip nothing else happened. But when they got inside the cove, it was time for action.

That was because Amas and his eight henchmen were standing right before us!

"Well, I guess we'll just have to fight 'em." I said.

"Yeah." Dylan assured me, turning to Amas and his henchmen.

"But," I thought, "Our fight may or may not last for more than four hours." That was dinnertime.

Getting back to the point, I planned to do a cool move. It was, because it was successful, thank you for the railing.

I did a pull up on the railing, then putting my feet on another rail. He was in front of me, turned around facing Dad. When my feet let go, I was still holding on with my hands. I was swooping downwards toward Bob 2.

"Look out below!" I shouted.

Dad moved because he saw me, but Bob 2 didn't fall for it. Or did he? He must have thought it was a joke.

Know what? I never thought a bad guy like that could be so, jerky. He rammed into the side of the cove. Some pebbles and small rocks fell on him and he was dead.

"That was easy!" I thought. Dylan did a cool move, just as I did. He hopped onto the railing and smashed the bad guy who had just walked to stop under him. He did not die, but was very weak.

"Scores for moves?" Dylan asked.

"Oh, no, no, no, no, no, no, no, no, there's way to many people here to do that." I disagreed.

There were some mutters and mumbles from the others from under their breaths, "Good point."

After that, Dylan said, "I was just joking."

They walked on with Dylan saying, " Cell 4, 8, 12, Cell 16, 20, 24, 28, 32…"

One hour later, Dylan was still counting, " Cell 2574, 2578, 2582, Cell 2586, person in 2590, 2594, person in 2590!" Everyone stopped in their tracks.

50

Then, Dad shouted from far ahead, "Person in 2618 and 2624!" "Dad, Dylan, and I will check initials for 2618! Gibbins, Bradey, Roger, Bobby! Go for 2590! And Sammy, Marty, Mary, Kim! Go for 2624!"

I directed, "The initials we're looking for are A.A.!"

"B.C.!" Dad shouted.

"Z.D.!" Roger shouted.

"E." -- Sammy started but I interrupted -- "A clue!"

I started as I picked it up, then finished, "In cell *67   A.A.*" "We should be getting back, shouldn't we? And besides, we already found a clue to where Adam is."

"Well..." I stretched, "I guess so." As the others came out, Amas and his friends got up.

"Uh-oh." Kim said. But, the boys had a plan as quick as a snap. They would untie the boat, Tony would rev it up, while the others were distracting Amas.

They also knew that it was a dangerous, and desperate escapade. But it was the only way out. Sure it would work, it was foolproof! It worked and apparently we actually left them stranded on the cove! Surely enough, the boys were pooped.

When Mom saw, she said, "You boys wear out you're energy too much. You know, it's not like you have invincible energy. In fact, you boys need more sunlight. It gives you the Vitamin D and energy to do things. Go get yourself a bike or something."

Why they did not have a bike was not a mystery. They had one at age nine. Now it did not fit. Now they had a chance to get one. So, as soon as they had enough energy to walk and steer, they grabbed all the money in their piggy banks and set off to a bike shop named *Advanced Pedals* where they had a sale.

After percents and taxes and totals, the boys soon knew that the price was $100.80. They needed helmets - and cash. But, they knew they had enough- $38.20.

What I didn't know was if Dylan would waste it all on his helmet, for I had most of the cash. After helmets, the boys had $1.00 left. By the time we got home, it was 5:13.

We packed. Dylan was still a bit grumpy, for the memory of the lost race at the terminal took over his mind.

"Now, when I get back, I wish to hear about success." Dad warned.

"We won't give you failure, sir." I teased, "It'll be in the paper that *they* failed."

"That's my boys." Dad said. As the plane waited for the boys, the checkup was sure to start. By the time the boys got there, the plane had been cleaned, checked, waxed, ready, they even took the scratches off from last time's accident.

As soon as they got *inside* the plane, they learned it was comfortable and even vacuumed.

"Wow, Chris, your plane has totally changed for good!" I complimented.

"Thanks." Chris accepted, then continued, "What's your destination this time, boys? Africa? Asia? -- I answered -- "Chi" -- Dylan interrupted, answering the more exact answer -- "Nepal."

We took off and on their way. By 11:02, we were in Mauritania, Africa. As I look down, I was glad to see something different. I didn't even want to be going to Orlando, not even Las Vegas.

I was finally on a smooth trip, not Dylan bragging about all the games he wins in Las Vegas, or even him bugging about getting on a ride (especially Mt. Everest) in Orlando.

Since Dylan was asleep, there was no ruckus from him. I eventually fell asleep, too. The next morning at 2:45, I was up, but apparently Dylan woke up ten minutes earlier.

We landed 15 minutes later, got our rental car, and got out. Dylan was no longer angry anymore because of the relaxing trip.

"Kyle, do you notice the differences between New York and Nepal?" Dylan asked.

"Well duh?" I answered, "And I'm hungry."

"What are we going to eat? A local *Chinese-American* open 24 hour McDonald's? There is nothing to eat." Dylan said with a pinch of sarcasm.

"I was just saying." I said, still driving, but not pulling over to climb in the back seat to get him. The Chinese government could have passed a law saying, 'Do not pull over to do something that is not very serious.'

When we got to the hotel we were pretty useless, until the 5:00 news came on.

The newsman said, "For the forecast of tonight, it will be very foggy, so put your headlights on, and especially, watch what you are doing. About 73 for 6:00, 65 for 12:00, and 71 at 5:00 tomorrow" – then I turned the TV off.

"Did you hear that?"

"No." Dylan answered.

"Foggy and cold for twelve. So we'll be bringing jackets, and also, be looking even harder because of heavy fog. Can't believe there are so many disadvantages, but no advantages. I just don't get it."

"Oh, well. We'll find out when we get there at twelve." I said.

"Yeah. I hope it's not too foggy to see them." Dylan said.

"What are you looking at anyway?" I asked.

"Chris." Dylan answered.

"Why?" I asked.

"Think of his name. Doesn't it sound like – a fake or something?" Dylan answered.

"Well... kinda." I said, "Well, then, why would he want to fly us to Nepal? He'd be trying to get us off track if he were a criminal." Then they had a big argument.

"Look at this webpage!" Dylan blurted, "Right here! He belongs to Alan Strovenki's gang!"

"They're a Japanese gang?!" I was confused, but kept on reading anyway, "Chris flew to America in 2000. Then he learned how to fly, in case there was an emergency on his way back. He has never returned to Japan, for he has had lessons to speak English, and took a job of flying charter planes, so he would not look suspicious. Then came Kyle and Dylan Hamer, his worst enemies. Dylan and Kyle better be careful, because I hear he is going to sock them!"

"We'll do that." I said partly to the webpage and partly to Dylan.

By then it had been an hour later. After at least twenty minutes of flipping channels among nine hundred fifty-four out of one thousand of them, they finally found something they liked on Channel 4. The Adventures of Kooky Kangaroo and Smart Squirrel (Episode 217)

"Come on!" I called.

What was he doing this time? He was going to drop a pickup truck of marshmallows on Smart Squirrel. But Kooky Kangaroo's crane was broken. Front went back. Back went front. Left went right. Right went left. You get the point. When he thought it was over the squirrel, it was over him.

Apparently, he didn't build a cover on it. So, when he pressed drop, it went on him. After the show, it was 9:00. 45 minutes later, the boys set off.

It took a teensy-weensy bit over an hour to get there. Then, they waited for 15 minutes. After that, a helicopter came into the boys' view.

Then, I heard a voice, "We need a plan that is very elite for Kyle and Dylan. We will surely get Kyle, but that Dylan just might survive. Then, we will scare him off the face of the Earth. We could use a robot. Maybe 'Detective Destroyer Level 1'. But we would have to build it." Amas said.

"Bob's got a tool shed in his backyard. He wouldn't mind, I bet. And I've got metal at my house. We could use that. All we need is a metal cutter, which we could steal from the hardware store." Bob II said.

"Great idea. I'll think about it." Amas said. Then, the helicopter flew away. I assumed Amas was going to decide in the helicopter.

"We better be very cautious." Dylan warned me.

"And not tell anyone about it. You can even cross out Dad on our list, if you know what I mean."

By morning, the boys were ready to fight anything. Meanwhile, Amas was working on the plans for the robot, finishing at 3:17. At 4:00, the boys decided to steal the plans.

"We need a plan." I said.

"How 'bout taking the fire hoses, shooting up to the top of the tree, and since the metal shouldn't be thick, we can pop his head off. Then, one of us takes both hoses and uses one as a jetpack, one as a fire hose. Then, the one of us sprays the inside of him. Robots hate water. He's gonna die from it. It's only a level one. Wrong! Level... oh, I don't know."

The next day, the robot was done and set. They set it out. We got there. I leaped to the fire hose, grabbing it by the nozzle. Dylan followed on the opposite side. Then, clenching the handle, pulled the head. Taking turns, they had almost defeated him.

"I was wrong. This is a level" -- I was cut off because the level 10 was swinging his arm directly at me! We just needed to hose him a bit more and he would be finished!

Then, a miracle happened. He smacked himself once, flicked himself once, and poked himself three times! All that together... shut the robot down.

"So, what was the level?" Dylan asked. "This'll answer your question." I answered. I had found a chart.

"0.1 equals 1?" Dylan was confused. "They're trying to trick us." I said. "Aha! So this was a chart of levels. And this was... evidence! Proof!

"Now we can tell Dad!" I said.

Meanwhile, in Amas' control room, Amas said, "Drat! They both survived!"

Kyle and Dylan headed back to America. There weren't any mishaps back to America, except for running out of gas in France. At home, the boys were a bit shaky to tell Dad. But they did anyway.

"Dad, we have something to -- just then the phone rang. I slid over to the phone in case it was danger. It was Marty.

"Come over here quick!" he said.

"What is it?!" I said frantically. Then there was static.

"Uh-oh! We're breaking up! I'll tell you at the house." Then the static and Marty had hung up.

"Quick! To the convertible! Marty is in trouble!" I said, now worriedly.

At Marty's house, he was giggling.

"What are you laughing about?" I asked quizzically.

"The static-fake!" Marty was practically speaking gibberish in that sentence. We were silent.

"Don't you get it? I took a job as a ventriloquist!"

"And you've probably got a job for us. What's next- digging," -- I said but Marty interrupted -- "Cleaning! The house has been ransacked! And I have only got a day 'til my parents get back! I will never get finished in time!" Marty freaked.

"Don't worry. After Hawaii, we sent them to Las Vegas for a week. But before you start, we'd like to dust for fingerprints." I said.

After dusting a few rooms, I said, "Whoever did it was wearing gloves." Then there was a sharp pencil in the wall. Then, at the tip, we all saw it. *A glove!*

"Everyone in Amas' gang is right-handed, right?"

"Except Amas and Bob 2."

"Great! Amas must have sent someone else besides Bob 2 because he is the weakest in case he would have to face anyone. So, from here on, we should find fingerprints on the doorknobs!" I said excitedly.

And I was correct.

Later, Dylan asked, "But if we know Amas didn't do it, and we don't have fingerprints of all the gang, then how are we going to find out who did it?"

"Instead of getting fingerprints, how about when you get the gang, you could interrogate them." Marty said, sounding like Kyle.

"Good thinking, Kyle." Dylan said.

"I didn't say that." I said.

"Then who did?" Marty started laughing.

"I did!" he said.

"Good job, Mr. Ventriloquist." I teased. Nothing else was found. After an hour of cleaning, we went home.

At the car, I said, "I want to solve Marty's mystery before ours. It could give us a lead to follow."

"Well, if you want it that way, I guess I should confess. I had figured out the puzzle as soon as I knew his house was ransacked." Dylan confessed.

"What?!" Dylan thought I was insane and he continued, "I should have told you. Scott Turner lives exactly three blocks from Marty."

Scott Turner is one of Amas' henchmen. He has a history of criminal activity.

"531 Maple, 561 Maple. You're right!" I compared, "He would be right on-hand for a ransacking!"

"He surely did it. I'm not positive, for it is only a suspicion." Dylan said.

"I could have figured that out on my own!" I said.

"That's the whole reason that I *didn't* tell you." Dylan said.

Chapter VI
Failures

DYLAN

Instead of leaving, we got out of the car to tell Marty. When we got inside, he was still working on the living room. It had been ransacked the most.

"Back so soon?" Marty said exhaustedly.

"You need to tell your parents that they need to move." I said.

"What! Why?" Marty was out of control.

"I'll explain it for you." Kyle said, "Scott lives exactly three blocks from you. He is the one who ransacked the house. If you don't move, the threats will probably become worse. But, do not move to Jefferson Street, Easy Street, Fare Street, Elm Street, which is our street, Willow Lane, Harper Street, A Avenue, 15th Street, or Jamaame Dr."

"Why can't I live with you?" Marty asked.

"Because, then it could cause more trouble added to what Amas and his gang have done already." I answered logically, and out of breath.

Feeling intimidated, Marty said, "Well, I guess I can move." Then, the boys left, assuring themselves that their minds were vacant of anything else to tell Marty. As soon as we got to 557 Maple Street, Scott, Jane, Bob 1, and Bob 2 jumped out from bushes and grabbed them.

Scott and Jane had me and both Bobs had Kyle. Then we argued all the way about who caused us to be captured in the first place. Then when we got to Amas' base, they put us in separate rooms. I was fighting 5 level 4s. They were able to morph themselves!

After calculations, I thought, "If all 5 morph, it'll be a level 200! Then it will be almost impossible without Kyle. Maybe even with him it will be still almost impossible."

Meanwhile, Kyle was fighting 30 level 1s. They were able to morph also. They made a ladder shape. Kyle defeated a 0.1 by stepping on it.

When I stepped on the 0.5, Amas came along and said, "What idiot is controlling them?!" He grabbed the control and unmorphed the robots. I had to jump to grab the fire hose. Then, Kyle inched his way to the nozzle, which was not far. Then, Kyle rode down.

Then he heard it. "Help!" I was saying.

"My brother needs help, and I'll help him." I thought. I sprayed the 23 and busted open the door. They were morphing into a level 200!

After calculations, it would take 6700 fire hose sprays to do it. So, I took off the head and plunged into cords. Then, I pulled a cord. It only needed 5350 sprays now. Then, I pulled more cords. Down sprays went. 5215, 5210, 4990, 3490, 1365, 1280, 280, 205, 55, 30, 29, 4, 3, 2, 1, dead. I had jumped out at four. Back in the other room, a level 100 *and* two 50s were waiting.

Thank goodness they were not able to morph. However, I was stuck with a 800. I'll start with me this time.

You couldn't pop his head off, so I took my pocketknife out of my right pocket. It cut 10 cords. Then it only had 13185 life points left. I didn't go by sprays. I didn't have my pocketknife, so I couldn't do anything else.

Just then, Marty drove by us. Then I heard banging glass. Kyle. I couldn't rap on the window like Kyle because the level 800 was after me.

Then, suddenly, Marty looked our way. Before I knew it, he was glaring at us helplessly. Then, he had planted an idea. He walked around and into the door, made his way to the controls, and pressed self-destruct for the level 800, 100, and the two fifties.

Amas had seen enough. He went to the controls.

"I hope Marty planned this." I thought. Marty whirled around to the other side of him. He punched him in the face, knocking him into the controls. His elbow accidentally pressed the 'release' button. We came out and helped Marty with Amas. Three seconds later, knocked out.

Bob 2 stood at the door. I knocked Bob 2 out while Kyle and Marty busted out the door.

At the car, Marty said, "The house is cleaned up. I decided to find a cheap motel here. You're very lucky people, you know."

"We have decided that we should give approvals on where you should go." I said.

"Okey-dokey." After a couple hours, Marty dropped them off at their house.

"What an adventurous trip." I said.

When they got inside, Aunt Gertrude shrieked, "Look at yourselves! Go take a bath! Something that at least involves cleaning yourselves!"

I had to agree. Ripped T-shirts, torn jeans, socks with holes in them, even the laces were coming off our shoes, and everywhere, filth.

After 30-minute showers, I said, "Another escape with no clues."

"I believe you're mistaken." Kyle corrected me by holding up one, "I found it while you and Marty were fighting Amas."

It looked like:

FI HSTI TMPATET EODS
TON RKOW XNTE ILWL
EB TA WTON. SLVELE:
3185, 4278, 7236, DAN
8614.

"IF THIS ATTEMPT DOES NOT WORK, NEXT WILL BE IN TOWN. LEVELS: ... Hmmm. I don't know what the levels are." I said.

"I don't either." Kyle said, still both confused.

"Let's watch the news." I said, flipping to channel 3.

"Someone has stolen a crane from Presque Island Crane Storage..." the news reporter said.

"Amas." Kyle suspected.

"To Presque Island!" I said loudly. I had brought my mini-television with me, so, I was watching the news on the way.

Then it came on. Amas had done it again. With a tow truck. Five minutes later, we came across a tow truck with a crane on it.

"That's Amas! Follow him!" I commanded. We were on the highway. On the way to Augusta.

To the most famous building in Maine, the capitol building. Amas was swinging the boulder ten feet from the building!

I quickly shoved Amas out of the crane, pulling back, turned around, and knocked Amas' building packed with his minions. Amas' minions evacuated just in time.

Kyle came in for the grand finale which was the rest of Amas' building with minions. After that was done, they stayed in the crane, waiting for the owner. The owner was in his office.

He noticed the crane was back and notified WCBB, WNBC, WABC, WCBS, WYNE, WPIX, WWOR, WUTR, WAGM, and WMEM.

WCBB arrived first.

"Mr. Hamer, did you expect to successfully negotiate this attempt?" WNBC said.

"How does it occur to you that Amas is still full blast in his own attempts?" WUTR said.

They were sinking in questions.

"Quiet!" I shouted, "One at a time, please. We cannot answer twelve questions at once."

A line was formed, WNBC starting it. Then WAGM. Then WCBS. WPIX, WMEM, WUTR, WNYE, WWOR, WABC.

Questions were asked. After that, we went home and Kyle went to bed, but I stayed up.

After hours and hours of working on the unscrambling the code, I finally said, "I've got it!" Kyle jolted from his covers.

"What?" he said. "I know the levels. Come over here." I was blinded at first, but got used to the light.

"They are 3185, 4278, 7236, and 8614." Dylan said.

"It's 2:00 in the morning and you got this?"

"Well, yeah." Dylan confessed.

Just then our six-year-old brother Tommy walked into the room. I sighed. "You... bed. You... watch."

Five minutes later, we heard a rustling sound in the bushes. "Amas. Hide!" I said.

Tommy came along saying, "What's happening?"

"Bed." I commanded.

A few minutes later, Amas was in their room. Amas found us and tied us up.

Then, Tommy came sliding into the room whispering loudly, "As much as I know not to spray water guns in the house, this is for a reason. He sprayed pepper spray into his eyes. I could tell it burned badly because he was screaming.

Tommy sprayed once more after pushing him to the window in our bedroom, and Amas stumbled into the window.

"I can't take anymore of this pepper spray!" Amas said, and ran off. Tommy walked over to the boys and untied the rope.

"You could become a professional detective yourself." I complimented Tommy on his skills.

"I guess I won't be sleeping on my hands tonight." Dylan said.

"Back to bed, everyone." I commanded, then said, "Oh, and, Tommy, just because I told you that you *could* become a pro, don't think that you can follow us tomorrow. Because tomorrow we are going on a very dangerous mission."

"O.K." Tommy said.

"You can help on the investigations and searching, but leave the fights to us." I reminded him.

Then, I turned off the lamp and went to sleep.

KYLE

The next morning at 8:00, we went to the park with Roger, Bobby, Kim, Mary, Gibbins, Bradey, Sam, and Marty. The park was full. *Until...* A level 1385 robot, 2478 robot, 3726 robot, and 4816 robot came into the park.

"Rope." I said to Marty. As soon as he gave me the twine, I grappled to the top of the robot, lit a stick of dynamite and threw it in.

That destroyed 25,225 life points out of 62,325 life points. Then, everyone roped his feet and tied it to a 1000 lb. weight, which was on a conveyer belt. It dragged the robot toward its air curtain in the middle. The parts would come off eventually, so they headed on up. I grappled from the top of the play set and dropped a bomb by his feet. It was a close escape, but he made it.

The robot died.

Now for the 3726. After a death-defying battle with it, the 4816 was all that was left.

During the battle with the 4816, Dylan broke his leg, so I screamed to Roger, "Get Dylan to the hospital! We will be there as soon as we can!"

After finishing off the robot with some of our best moves, we ran to the hospital (because Roger and Dylan had taken the car).

When we got there Dylan was in bed. "Wow, that was a quick procedure." He said.

"He's been out for four hours." Roger whispered into my ear. I giggled.

"What's so funny?" Dylan asked.

"You're clueless aren't you?" I said. Roger started to giggle and I burst out laughing.

"Dylan, you have been out for over four hours!" Then everyone laughed. Dylan had to admit, it was a little funny.

Then I realized. This is not all fun and games. Time to get serious.

"Anyway, since Dylan's staying here, Marty, you're my new assistant until the doctor says its okay to get back to his own life. Tommy will be helping.

"Why him?" Bobby asked.

"Because -- he beat Amas last night when we were tied up tight." Dylan sounded very weak. For the rest of you -- you're gonna have to go undercover."

Then, I walked slowly to the door. "Now, I'm going home. Nobody disturb me either. You'll be alright alone, right?" I said.

"Don't worry. My parents don't expect me home for a few hours. I'll watch him." Kim said.

"Okay." I said, and left.

When I got home, Tommy was playing with his new toy truck.

"Where's brother?" Tommy asked.

"Well," I said, sitting down, lifting Tommy up and put him on my lap, "He's hurt and had to go to the hospital. But to cheer you up, I have a surprise!"

"Yeah! What is it? What is it? What is it?!" Tommy couldn't wait.

"Well, since Dylan is in the hospital, you can be one of my assistants!"

"Yeah!"

"But don't tell Mom, Dad, or Aunt Gertrude, okay? And don't be too happy about it. Dylan's still in the hospital, assistant or not. "

"Okay." Tommy agreed.

As long as he was an assistant he would not tell anyone.

"Now, let's go to the hospital and comfort brother." I said. After talking, I felt a little guilty. That night, I dreamt about being in court.

I woke up, frightened.

"I had the weirdest dream last night." I said.

Then I grabbed Tommy and left for the day. He was scared at first, but finally got used to it.

Chapter VII
More Bad Guys

KYLE

Meanwhile, at the hospital, Amas showed up. "What are you doing here?" Dylan said, holding out his fists.

"Whoa, whoa, I come in peace." Amas said.

"I doubt that." Dylan thought.

"But…" Amas pointed, "Since you won't be going anywhere for the next few weeks, I'm taking your brother down."

"You wouldn't dare." Dylan said.

"I'm a bad guy, what did you expect?" Amas said.

"Ooouuuttt!" Dylan shouted. Dylan called me.

"You didn't bring your phone, and you can't get out of bed, so, how are you calling me?" I asked.

"Oh, you left yours on the side-table next to me." Dylan answered.

"So that's where it went."

He said, "Amas is on to you. You need to -- I interrupted -- "Hang on, better yet, bye. This could take a while."

I bolted out of the door.

"Amas." I thought when I saw him. He was running until he jumped into a car as I jumped in mine. I chased him on the highway until he turned on to a road that led to a four-way intersection.

The GPS for Amas from the police was dying, plus he didn't have any more batteries. But, he barely saw a dot going west just before it died. So, he turned left. The road led to the New York City Superdome.

Inside a 500-lap race was going on. I couldn't find Amas, so, what the heck, why not watch it? They were on the 399th lap. I found Amas after the race. Then, the chase *was on*. He ran to the cave.

I hid on top of the cave, unnoticed. Then, I peered inside. Amas touched a panel on the cave, then he flipped a switch.

About a thousand panels (in the distance) slid open revealing lights. The second switch came through as a conveyer belt.

"That would have helped." I mumbled.

Unluckily, Amas heard me and stepped on a button near the ground.

Then, I pondered in my head. "What would it do to me? Would it hurt me? Would it kill me?" Suddenly a panel slipped from under me.

I collapsed, handling a nearby railing.

"Well, well, well. What do we have here." Amas said as I jumped off the railing.

I put out my fists for attack. "If you fight me, you'll have to have to go through the" -- Five cars drove up. Inside were Marty, Kim, Mary, Bobby, Roger, Dad, Dylan, and Sammy!

Amas sent radio-active robo-men out to kill them. When they were out, we started to fight.

Everyone except Dad and Dylan ducked and yanked a sword out of the robot's hands. Dad was too tall to duck the swords, and Dylan had crutches in his hands for his broken leg.

Dylan used his crutches for attack instead of struggling with a sword. Dad used his fists for a sword. As they say, his fists are metallic punches.

We fought for hours as Aunt Denise began to worry. As I fought, I wondered about how long the fight would be. It was 2:00 a.m. when we finally got a break.

"Worn out already? I've got plenty more." Amas said.

"How many of these does he have?" I asked myself.

This time the robots had guns instead of swords. Yes! Amas' forces were weakening! Then, sixteen robots surrounded me and all were firing. Hoping it would work, I ducked. The gunshots collided aiming back at the robots.

It killed the robots.

I glared at Amas' hand pushing the button for more to come. I wondered. Could this go on forever…?

Chapter VIII
The Missing Millionaire is Found

DYLAN

I thought as I dueled the robots. I needed to find a way to get through the robots and into the cave without Amas noticing.

"But how?" I thought. I fell down in my daydream and felt something cold and hard buried in dirt and rust.

It was a secret passageway.

"This must have been here for years!" I whispered loudly to myself. I opened the door quietly, went in, and closed it.

No robots came with me, so I was safe. I tiptoed until I thought Amas could not hear me. The other side of the hatch was very far from Amas.

Five minutes later, I saw initials. *They were A.A.! Adam Aksaw! The missing millionaire!* I studied the bars of the cell.

"Electric bars." I discovered.

A cracking sound interrupted my concentration. The millionaire fell down into the bottom cell.

"That thing could not have lasted another second anyway." The millionaire said.

Lucky for him, I had a little experience from working with a locksmith back in Bayport. It took a couple of minutes but we cracked the lock.

"You must be hungry." I guessed.

"In fact, I am. I have been eating stale bread and water for food. I am lucky to be alive." the millionaire said. I had been right.

"Then go get some food." I said.

"I'm broke." Adam said. I laughed intensively, pausing to think after a moment.

"You're kidding, right?"

"No, I'm not. Amas took all my money." Adam said. I sighed.

"Here's" -- I was cut off by the sound of marching. I whirled.

Robots! I gave the sword I had to Adam.

"I'll get another one." I said.

We fought with all our wits when I got another sword. All of the commotion drew the other robots out of the courtyard into the cave with us.

"A little help here!" I shouted.

Marty, Bobby, Roger, Mary, Kim, and Sammy came in as a bystander walked by the courtyard.

When that bystander saw the battle, he ran. Wait! Dad! He was missing!

When I asked Kyle, he said Roger was with him.

"Ask him." I managed to say.

"Bad news," said Kyle, "He does not know where Dad is either!"

Chapter IX
The Stampede

KYLE

"Boy we're dead meat without Dad." Dylan said.

"Hush!" I said. I had heard some kind of stampede. I turned around and was shocked to see an estimate of twenty-five million people in one enormous group! I jerked Dylan to the cave wall.

"What are you doing?" Dylan asked. I pointed out into the courtyard.

"Okay." Dylan said confusingly.

As soon as the mob came, we tiptoed out into the courtyard. "Look!" Dylan said suddenly. Bob 1 and Bob 2 were having a meeting. I tuned my attention to the river.

James and Joshua were having a meeting. Dylan looked in the direction I was looking in.

"Well then, let's synchronize our watches to 250 minutes for you, but mine only does seconds, so I do 1500 seconds, and really scrutinize their actions thoroughly, too." I decided.

"If a 4816 can brake Dylan Hamer's leg, then a 9,632 can kill him. Then a 2481 can spawn at the same time. That oughta kill Kyle Hamer and his idiot friends."

DYLAN

"Albert Hamer's gone in cell 7485.67."

That was all I had to hear.

I went back to the spot we were supposed to meet.

KYLE

"They're gonna spawn a 2481 and a 9632 on all of us!" I relayed my information to Dylan.

"Dad is in cell 7485.67." Dylan said, taking his turn.

".67?" I was confused.

"Let's just start at cell 7485." I said. Dylan started running to the cave, but I held him back.

"I know a shortcut." I said, "It'll get us to cell 7500."

I went to the hatch and opened it. We got there and found 7485. Dylan fell into a hatch. I jumped down into it.

We found Dad and broke him free so we could finally go home.

Chapter X
The Biggest Battle

KYLE

"Where have you been?!" Aunt Denise scolded, "It has been a week since I've seen you three. I was worried sick!"

"Sorry, Aunt Denise, we just went on a trip." I lied, stepping on Kyle's foot.

"To Maine." Kyle added, bent to tie his shoe, but ended up rubbing his toes anyway.

"Father, son meeting!" Albert said, changing the subject. In our room, Dad said, "What happened when I was gone? All the important information, anyway."

"The only thing I found out was where you were." I said.

"I'm not telling anything until everyone (except Aunt Denise) is here." Kyle said.

"Marty/Mary's number is: 785-439-187. Roger's is 786-137-4155. Bobby's number is 785-847-7457. Kim's phone number is 785-984-1691." I said.

"And Sammy's coordinates are 120 degrees (latitude) and 60 degrees (longtitude)." Kyle said.

"Which is somewhere in Canada." I inferred.

I had to plug the two-way radio to the wall (it doesn't get long-distance unless it is plugged into a wall socket).

"Sammy -- back -- Bayport -- urgent" -- it cut off at that moment.

"Man, I knew this thing couldn't go as far up as Canada. This thing has been here for years." I stated.

Two hours later, everyone was here.

"I want everyone to know what I've learned. There will be a robot with a level of twenty-four thousand, eight hundred ten and a level nine thousand, six hundred thirty-two heading for all of us." I announced.

"Well, count me out!!" Marty said loudly, but low enough to where Aunt Denise could not hear.

"Well, you're lucky. All you gotta do is bring your transportable hatches to the battle arena, then throw us unlighted dynamite continuously until we say 'stop'. Got it?" I said.

"Yep." Marty wasn't scared anymore.

"Okay, then let's go to the park!" Kyle said, not afraid of the robots. Everyone agreed.

At the park, robots leveled 24810 and a 9632 were waiting. At Amas' hangout, the robots who were controlling the other robots were impatient and left.

So, the robots were still and everyone had a chance of winning. Just then Marty arrived with all of his transportable hatches to the battlefield.

"Dynamite!!" I shouted across the park. I even held the matches in the air. Marty was now throwing. I threw the dynamite rapidly at the level 24810 robot.

But the robot's power was too strong for the group. It disintegrated the dynamite into a pile of pitch black ashes.

"It's disintegrating them! We have no hope!" Kyle shouted.

"I wouldn't let *that* hypnotize me, but take cover!" I then shouted.

Everyone ducked to the nearest picnic table. Since the robot did not notice them, they were all safe.

"Here's the plan. Marty, you walk to the other picnic table and wait for a five second period, then walk to your hatches and get: 2 swords, 4 guns, 2 grapplers, 20 pieces of dynamite, 40 grenades, and 30 thermal detonators. Give Albert and Sammy each 20 grenades and 15 thermal detonators. Give Roger and Bobby 2 guns each. Give Kyle and I each 1 grappler and sword. And that's all. Mary, go for the 24810 and Kim go for the 9632. I will go to the play area and grapple to Concession Stand A. Then B. Then the robot. Kyle, you will grapple to C, and then grapple to the robot. Roger, you will take place at A and shoot the robot. Bobby same for you, except at C. Sammy and Dad, plant detonators and throw grenades at both robots."

"Now, does everyone know their plan?" I asked. Everyone nodded.

"Marty, go" I stretched the word, "Now!" Marty set off, hid, and was there. I fired a signal for Mary and Kim to go.

Then me and Dylan, then Roger and Bobby and Albert and Sammy. I set off. Everything went as planned until I was in the robot. A panel like at Amas' hideout?

Weird, but ridiculous. It read 1564 x 5 + 513 - _____ = 1111. I thought, "Well, 1564 times 3 =7820 add 513 minus 5000 and you get 1111!"

I was in. I slashed cords and the robots life points were going down. I could tell because of a device that Dad got for me on Christmas last year.

I read life points and they were going down as I cut each cord. It read: 74430, 74280, 74130, 73980, 73830… that was four millionths of all of the cords. After ten minutes it read 61830.

Then a sign in brick red read: **DANGEROUS CORDS. YOU WILL BE ELECTRECUTED IF TOUCHED.**

"But the grappler won't!" I thought. I ripped the cords out with the grappling hook.

"Thank goodness the grappling hook is not a conductor." I said out loud. I noticed from the device that the dangerous cords were worth 500 life points.

There were 75 cords that were dangerous. After depleting those the robot had 24330 life points left.

After 20 minutes, I saw that the robot had 30 life points left, so I kicked a loose panel for escape.

Bobby shot the last fire and the robot blew up behind me.

KYLE

I slashed wires wildly. I had slashed 15 wires. I did not have a gizmo like Dylan, so I was subtracting in my head. 28896-150-150-150… to get 26645.

Then a sign read: **DO NOT TOUCH THESE WIRES.**

Then Dylan shouted, "The ones you can't touch are worth 500 life points! Use your grappler!"

I did so. There were 50 wires. Then there were only 1645 life points left.

"I'll leave the rest to Roger." I decided, making my way to the top.

I jumped out and leaped to the swing set railing as the robot was blowing up.

"And not a scratch on us!" Dylan said gleefully.

DYLAN

"Let's get some chow!" Marty suddenly realized that he was hungry, "My last meal was 4 hours ago and I could be dead!"

I giggled, "You were safe. Everyone else – could be dead – all you did was throw gizmos and weapons!"

Marty was embarrassed, but defended himself by saying, "Well, I bet you're hungry, at least!"

Everyone agreed, but a giggle exasperated Marty.

At the restaurant, Kyle suddenly said, "Look! There's Amas!"

"Well, what a coincidence." Dad said. Marty was scared.

"Aw, snap out of it. You're the one who picked this restaurant, so quit complaining." I slapped him on the back.

Amas looked our way, but we ducked just in time. We got up and Amas never checked our way again, so we ate happily.

Everyone nodded enthusiastically when Marty suggested ice cream. After that, everyone went home.

"Well, I never get a break, I suppose." Aunt Denise complained dissatisfiedly.

"We'll give you a break later." I said with my own voice, "But right now we have some work to do."

In our room, I said, " I overheard that Amas and his gang are moving to Asia."

"Latitude: 45 degrees and longitude: 65 degrees." Kyle said. "You can't drive. It's over the Atlantic." I pointed out.

"We'll have to fly - if we can." I frowned disappointedly.

"Look, I'll double the pay you get doing odd jobs and chores." Dad said.

"OK!" we said gleefully.

"Break!" Kyle called, "We're going to Asia!"

"What!" Aunt Denise threw her hands in the air, "Are you crazy?! First you fight robots and now you expect me to let you go to Asia! What's next, going to Antarctica to fight Bigfoot?"

While Kyle started to wash dishes, I made a chart that looked like this:

_____ / Washing dishes/$2.00/$4.00
_____/Mowing Lawns/$10.00/$20.00

____/Painting/$25.00/$50.00
____/Weeding/$5.00/$10.00
____/Washing Cars/$3.00/$6.00
____/Fixing Computers/$35.00/$70.00 (per hour)

Just then, the phone rang. It was Marty. "Can you come over and fix this darn computer?"

"For seventy bucks, because we're going to Asia!" I said.

"What do you mean, *we*?" Marty asked. "As in me, Kyle and Dad!"

"Oh, ok." Marty said, then put in, "By the way, somebody called earlier, he said he was going to kill you, Kyle, me and our friends."...

Chapter XI
The Victims' Comeback

KYLE

"We're going to Marty's." Dylan said.

"Why?" I asked.

"Oh, his Internet is not working, and besides, he agreed to seventy dollars an hour, anyway. We need money." Dylan said, "Oh, and, bring the walkie-talkies. I have a feeling that we're going to need them."

At Marty's house, I knocked on the door and Marty greeted by saying, "Hello." But then after the greeting, he said, "Man, I've gotta report due tomorrow and my Internet's not working? Now that's a horrible start for a computer!"

"The first thing is to go to 192.135.103.62 to try to change properties of the Internet." I said as I typed it in.

"Can you change your IP number?" Marty questioned.

"I don't believe so." Dylan said. After trying to change properties for an hour and thirty-five minutes, I said, "I believe that it's not the computer, but it may be that the satellite dish is positioned in the wrong place. But may I have your tallest ladder?"

"Yeah, sure!" Marty exclaimed.

Marty disappeared then after called out, "It's outside when you're ready, Kyle!"

I walked outside and climbed the ladder, then said, "Guys, go inside and get me a walkie-talkie, then stay in so you can see if it is working or not."

"Ok!" Dylan said excitedly as if they were going to Asia, then proceeded to my command.

After my command to Dylan was complete, I started my mission by twisting and turning the satellite.

"Now?" I asked.

"No." Dylan answered.

"Now?"

"No."

"Now?"

"No."

"Now?"

"No."

"Stop asking! I'll tell you when the satellite is working!" Dylan screamed into the walkie-talkie.

After five minutes, something life-threatening happened with Amas at the middle of it.

Amas crept across the yard and stole the ladder. I was helpless, until... I had an idea. Morse Code! I tapped in .... . .-.. .--. .-.-.- and hoped that it would work.

Meanwhile at the time that I had started to tap on the roof, Dylan said,

"Hey! Listen! H-E-L-P. Help! Kyle needs help!" Dylan said frantically, but softly so no one could hear.

They rushed outside. I was hanging on to the satellite and gave it a twist right before the boys got me down. The Internet was working again.

"Well, that was two hours." Marty sighed, giving us the one hundred fourty dollars he owed us.

When we got home, again, Aunt Denise was unhappy, and said surprisingly, "Well, you're home! Do you think that I don't care! I mean, no note, no warning, nothing! For heaven's sake, boys, even the dishes were left unwashed!" Well, I didn't finish them, of course. -- then I interrupted -- "We'll get the dishes."

After twenty minutes of doing the dishes, we showed the chart to Dad. "Well, it sounds fine to me. Here's your one hundred fourty dollars since I'm doubling." then he lowered his voice to a whisper and said, "I can come along, and I will, so I'm going to triple the money for me."

"Gee, how do you get so much money being a private investigator?" I asked.

"It's just being popular, son, just being popular." he answered, giving me another stack of dollars.

"We are going to need one thousand dollars if you were counting hotels and all that other stuff. Who knows how much it could cost!" I said.

"You're right. And we have to be prepared." Dylan said. Then the telephone rang. I answered it immediately.

"Hello." I said. "I heard you would paint houses for $50 an hour and I think it is an excellent deal! Most people do it double! I have a house that will take 3 hours inside and out. You see, my wife had the house painted pink three years ago and I do not like pink. Well, she died and now I have the chance to repaint it." the man said.

"Information, please." I said.

"I'm Henry Lanes. I live on 485 Fareway Avenue and directions are from Easy Street to Doftin Drive to Fareway Avenue." Henry Lanes said.

"We'll be over there in a little while!" I said delightfully, then hung up and said to Dylan, "We're going to Asia!"

Then I related the phone call to him.

"Let's go!" Dylan said. We went to the Lanes' house and Henry answered.

"Well, hello. I have the paint waiting." he said.

"Aaah, I love those people. They get right to business." I said.

We painted in neat strokes for over three hours and Henry gave us $200.00 in cash.

"Why the extra fifty dollars?" I asked.

"Twenty-five for generosity and twenty-five for the other half-hour you painted. " Henry said.

As I drove, I said, "Well, that was a super de-duper luck wave! But save your energy and excitement. Something's telling me another one's coming... and soon!"

When we got to our house, I told Mom, "Well, we need two hundred dollars more to go to Asia!" Then Dad arrived and glanced at our faces.

"What did I miss?" he said.

"Only that... we're going to Asia!" I said, "We'll discuss it in our room."

"We got two hundred dollars. Since it's tripled, we get six hundred dollars!" I said when we got into our room.

"And I just solved another mystery! And I'm going to use at least one hundred seventy-five dollars to go to Asia."

"And that's one thousand dollars! Which is exactly how much we need!" I said jubilantly.

"Watch out Amas, here we come!" Dylan said.

After departing Bayport, I said, "Look! There's Amas!"

Amas was on the same flight to Asia.

"Then we are dead meat! Amas could see us any time! And this flight lasts 12 hours!" Dylan said disappointedly, "But, I hope he keeps distracted."

After a long flight, the intercom in the plane came on and the flight attendant said, "We are now landing in Asia."

"Trail Amas." I said. We trailed until Amas hailed a taxi.

"Oh, we can't do anything now." I sighed.

Well, I saw a piece of Amas' shirt hanging on a bush.

"This way!" I said loudly. Going down Hatskogil Lane, I told Dylan to follow the pieces of torn shirt.

Soon enough, there was a huge crowd in front of us, with Amas at the heart of it!

"Oh, great, we have only been in Asia for ten minutes, and he has this many victims?! What did he do, destroy a building?" Dylan said.

"Great theory." I said, and pointed to some smoke from which gas pipes that were broken had caused the detrimental scene. All of the remains were scattered everywhere. Then, a devastating scene took place. Amas threw a tear gas bomb.

I shouted, "Oh, no! We have got to evacuate the people... or else everyone, including us, will die!"

Chapter XII
Amas Strikes Again

DYLAN

"Evacuate!" I shouted, but no one listened, "Wait a second! Duh! No one understands our language."

Then, once we shouted in their language, they listened and evacuated.

"Go on!" I said, "I'll take care of Amas."

"What?! I'm going with you." Kyle refused.

"No! I'm going alone." I said and he fled towards Amas.

"Follow him." Kyle said.

Dad obeyed, which was normal. I dived for Amas and he fell to the ground with a thud.

"Why, you!" Amas said, struggling to try to escape my outstanding grip on him.

"Oh, no! He must've forgotten about the tear gas bomb!" Kyle said to Dad.

"Only if we can manipulate the power to a minimum, the projectile will not harm Dylan." Dad explained.

"You're correct!" Kyle said, "Let's do it."

When they got to the tear gas bomb, Kyle tore open the panel and started to push buttons rapidly.

Then he said with a frustrated sigh, "It's no use."

"Let me try." Dad said, pushing Kyle sideways.

After a few seconds, Dad said, "If only we had more time." Then a miracle occurred. Kyle spotted a time change button. Rapidly, but carefully, they changed the time to five minutes. Meanwhile, my strength weakened to ounces.

But, Kyle came flying like an airplane at Amas. Before I knew it, Amas was bruised from head to toe because of that move.

Beep, beep, beep… it went on and on.

"The bomb!" I shouted loudly, then Dad, Kyle, and I retreated.

"Say, did you minimize the power of the bomb?" I asked. "Nope! Still on maximum power."

Dad whispered embarrassingly, "Oops."

"If Marty would have been here, he would have taken the jet home immediately!" I teased, trying to change the subject, and it worked.

"Yeah." Dylan said, then laughed vigorously.

Then, the rest of the way, we walked silently and registered into a hotel.

"Room 896." the man said, but transferred into English. "Okay." I said to Kyle.

"Wait a second. Your accent. Are you the Hamer Boys?" the man asked.

"Yes." I said. "Then I have a message for you. It is from a Mr. Marty Lopez." the man said, but in English, and gave me an envelope.

Then we left the reception desk.

In our hotel room, I read Marty's letter aloud.

Dylan, Kyle, and Mr. Hamer,
It seems Amas has left his henchmen (Bob Pepito, Bob II, Jane Dunning, Joshua McCarthy, Scott Turner, James McGee, Parker Hebert, Bill Taft, Shooter Boudreaux, and the robots) behind on his trip to Asia. So, the others and I got together and started spying on them. We learned that Amas' weakness is the loss of money. So, we came up with a brilliant plan for you guys. In fact, it's almost impossible to fail. You see, Amas likes to keep his money in a safe. In the middle of the night, you go and steal the safe. Keep it somewhere until morning, then bust it open at dawn. Then, when Amas awakens, he will not suspect you've taken it. Also, I got on a treadmill these past few hours! I admit, I like it and I'll keep doing it two hours a day until I'm not overweight anymore.
> *Your friend,*
> *Marty*

P.S. I lost about 5.75 lbs. already and I haven't broken a sweat yet.

P.S.T. Everyone says hi, including me!

"Well, do you want to try out their plan?" I asked, "Because I do."

"I agree. If they took the time to make the plan for us, then we need to take the time to do the plan. Besides, they've done a lot for us. Especially the spying. So, they need the appreciation from us for what they have done." Kyle said.

"Well, I'll do it, if you don't make a speech like that again." I burst out laughing.

Even Dad giggled a bit, then said, "Okay, let's get to business." Four hours later, the plan went into action. I lowered a rope with Kyle on it, with Dad's help. This was not a one-man job, you know.

Kyle grabbed the safe with all of the money in it and yanked on the rope. We pulled Kyle up. We got to the hotel safely, and then into our room.

"Where can we hide this?" I asked.

"Top shelf of the closet." Dad instructed and I obeyed. In the morning, we destroyed the lock on the safe and opened the door. Millions of dollars were in there.

"Amas could have been a multi-millionaire with this!" I said excitedly.

"I know!" Kyle said, "We have to get this to Chief John in Bayport!" "But how?" I asked.

"Mail." Dad said.

"But it's not gonna fit in one envelope." Kyle rejected.

"Your right, but I didn't mean in an envelope, I meant a package." Dad corrected.

"Oh, okay." I said. We drove to the post office and got a 12 x 24 inch package. We decided to go to the hotel in case someone saw us and were suspicious that we were criminals.

We packed the money in the package, but then I thought of a theory, and said it out loud.

"Wait a second, what if this is counterfeit money?"

"Well, we can write and ask if he can determine that, and if it is real money, he should keep it safe." Kyle suggested.

"Now, that's a swell idea!" I said gleefully.

"Yes, I strongly suggest that we go with Kyle's suggestion." Dad said.

It was pretty complicated, but we got through the chain of words.

By this time, it was 11:30, lunchtime.

"Anybody want sandwiches?" I asked.

"Nah, I want red beans and rice." Kyle refused strongly. It was very tempting indeed, so I finally gave in.

"Okay!" I said. Eating, we had a conversation.

Then I spotted an eavesdropper listening to our conversation, but as soon as I spotted him, he left, so I didn't bother.

But then I thought, "What did he hear?" Then I just decided to not tell anyone. I noticed that Kyle was repeating my name. I turned his way.

Kyle asked, "What were you staring at?"

"Oh, nothing. Or at least I'd rather not tell you." I replied.

"Oh, come on… don't be a party pooper." Kyle said.

"Oh, all right." I just decided to give one word just in case, so I said, "Eavesdropper."

"What?! Where?!" Kyle shouted softly.

"Oh, I scared him off when I saw him, so stop being a whiney baby." I said. Just then the doorbell rang.

Everyone had finished breakfast, but I opened the door.

I said, "How may I help you?"

"Are you the Hamer Boys?"

"Yes, we are. Come in, please."

The man came in and sat down, then said, "I have a mystery for you. You see, someone has stolen the most valuable jewel in the world. I don't know anything, but I found a coded letter on the counter this morning." the man said.

It read:

1311417415 183 2084 1981817,
   119 251824 10141822, 12…

"Amas wouldn't write this long of a letter," I concluded, "It's a decoy!"

"It depends on how cruel it is." Dad rejected.

So, after translating, it read,

Manager of the shop,

As you know, I, Amas, have stolen the most valuable jewel in the world. The reason I stole the jewel is because I steal diamonds, jewels, and electronic stuff. I know this must be an abhorrent time for you, but then I thought, who cares! Ha!

Your death belongs to me,
Amas

P.S. If you Hamer Boys are reading this, you will die too.

"Now that we have read the letter, is there any way we can stop him?" the man said, then remembered, "Oh, how rude I was! I haven't even introduced myself! I am John Nathans, part English, part Asian."

Meanwhile, I was planning. "We have to lure Amas back to America, where there is a forty-seven state alarm for him.

Then we contact the chief to make it a fifty state alarm. Then the police will catch 'em. " I said.

"But how do we lure him?" John Nathans asked.

"We trick him into thinking that what he stole is not the most valuable jewel and that the most valuable jewel is in America." I replied, shutting all the blinds in the room.

"Let's get this plan into action." Kyle said, squinting his eyes as if he were evil.

"Tape recorder." I said, ignoring the scene.

I spoke into the tape recorder, saying, "You do not have the most valuable jewel, for the most valuable one is in Las Vegas, Nevada. Now, you must go, get the jewel!"

"Well, I never thought it would be that easy." John Nathans said.

"Oh, that was the easy part. Here comes the challenge. We have to place the recorder where Amas does not see it, just hears it." I said.

"But how will it know when to activate itself?" John Nathans asked. "It is motion activated." I conquered the problem before it started.

"But where is Amas now?" Kyle asked.

"He should be, according to my locator, on Herimn Street." Dad examined.

"Then we must go now." I calculated the time. We left and went straight to the elevator.

The elevator went: 8, 7, 6, 5, 4, 3, 2, L. We left immediately after we got into the lobby.

John, Dad, Kyle, and I traveled to a dark cave and now we were experiencing rain. We tiptoed into the cave. There was an enormous branch that poked into the cave and brought an idea to my head. "The tree!" I said loudly. I hid the tape recorder on a branch and put some leaves in front of it. We left silently without anyone noticing.

Back at the hotel, the receiver for the recorder started beeping loudly. We listened carefully. The broadcast went like this:

Recorder: You do not have the most valuable jewel, for the most valuable one is in Las Vegas, Nevada. Now you must go, get the jewel!

Amas: But that is in America.

"Oh, no! It's not going to reply!" I said.

"Actually, I put a walkie-talkie just in case." Kyle confessed, but it was a good one. "Talk into this one."

Then we continued the broadcast:

Walkie-Talkie: Do you want money and jewels or not?

Amas: Yes. You are right. I must go, and now!

"I think he left." I said, then I remembered instantly, "Contact the chief!" Kyle did so.

"Chief John, we need a fifty state alarm for Amas. He is heading for Nevada. No time to explain. Bye."

"Well, you could have had a conversation with the chief." I said passively.

"Well, I'd better get going. I have a job interview in an hour." John Nathans said, and left.

"Well, now that Amas is heading for Las Vegas, shouldn't we go too?" Kyle asked.

"Not exactly. We're going, but, we had just better act casual and play at the casinos." Dad said, and it was surprising that he had said that.

Then Kyle and I conversed about playing on the slot machines, and winning Texas Hold 'Em poker.

Because if you didn't know already, Las Vegas is the capital city of casinos.

I said, "Watch out Amas, here we come!"

Chapter XIII
One Capture

KYLE

Soon enough, we were almost ready for take-off on a Continental Airlines flight to Sacramento, California, then drive to Las Vegas, Nevada. This flight was longer because we were going from Bayport, New York and now we're going to Sacramento, California.

It was an adventurous journey. Dylan was asleep by the third hour. The trip took about twenty-three hours.

Dylan awakened, then asked, "Why the extra forty-five minutes?"

"Gas problem in Colorado." I replied. We spent an hour in Sacramento waiting to refuel.

Then we drove two hours to Las Vegas. We played slot machines and then we went into competition on who could win the most. I won 6-4. Then Dad and I tied on 7. Then I tried again. The machine had to have had a malfunction because I got about 503 quarters when I won the tiebreaker. That's $125.75 in cash! Then I was surprised at what I saw at the corner of my eye. It was Marty, Bobby, Sammy, Mary, Kim, and Roger!

"What you guys doing here, huh?" I asked confusingly.

"May I ask the same of you?" Marty asked.

"Well, I'd scram because Amas is here, in this casino. You see, we went with your plan, and made our own. We tricked Amas into stealing the most valuable jewel, and that it's here, in Las Vegas, in this casino. Now I hope I don't have to get more specific than that." I said.

Of course, Marty tried leaving, but Mary pulled him back. I don't blame her, she is his sister.

So I continued, "We need to stop him."

"And we will help." Sammy protested.

Just then, Dad and Dylan saw them and came over. "What did I miss?" Dylan asked, eying me closely like I was very guilty and suspicious of something I was not telling him.

"Nothing that you don't know already." I said.

"Yeah, just your situation." Kim added.

"Let's do this." They all put their hands in the middle. They raised their hands rapidly and shouted softly, 'Teamwork!'

I call it a success circle. We split into three groups. Group 1: Dad, Sammy, and Roger. Group 2: Dylan, Marty, and Mary. Group 3: Bobby, Kim, and me. Group one's job was to try to get what seemed the most valuable jewel. Group two's job: find clues.

My group's job? It was very dangerous, but we agreed.

Get Amas.

"Whistle loudly when you need us." Dylan announced to the others and me.

Dad was quite alarmed when he found out that you had to win a national poker game to get the jewel we were looking for.

"And there's only one person who could have a chance to win a poker game that big. Dylan."

DYLAN

Dad came over and asked me, "How would you like to take a break, let me take over, and you go play a game of national Texas Hold 'Em poker with the champions." I was oddly suspicious about what he said.

"I don't get it. Why?" I asked confusingly.

"Oh, all right. I give up. In order to get the jewel you have to win a game of national poker. And you're the only one we know who has a chance of winning.

"Okay then! In fact, we'll switch. I get the jewel, you find clues." I said excitedly. Everyone agreed. I was playing five minutes later. I was playing against seven opponents. I had two Aces. So, I bet two thousand dollars. Five bets of two thousand, not including me, one bet of twenty-one hundred, and one twenty-five hundred dollar bet. The pot: $16,600. Then they showed the flop. It was 8, 9, and King. After that, the turn was 8, 9, King, and 2. It was all up to this. If it was an Ace, I win. If not, I lose. Fortunately, it was an Ace.

The other player's hands were 3 and 4, 7 and 10, 5 and 7, 8 and 2, Jack and Queen, and Queen and 6. But, my new nemesis for poker had an Ace and a King. I won because an Ace is higher than a King.

Both of my friends were exhilarated and I, exhausted and excited, had $41,600! Unfortunately, my nemesis won the next round, but I only bet one hundred, which left me with $41,500. Third round. The last player was a lunatic putting all of his money in.

I had a King and a Jack. River: 4, 2, King, Jack, and 3. The crazy one lost, and I won by the crack of dawn, if you ask me.

Sixty-six thousand three hundred total! Six opponents left! The poker game went on for an hour when everyone but my nemesis and me were the only ones left.

The others were chipping their fingernails with their chattering teeth. I was nervous. Very nervous.

Or as Kyle would say, 'the indescribable apprehensive feeling'. I describe that phrase as 'unbreakable fear'. My opponent was grinning evilly. I had an Ace and a King. The bet was three thousand dollars. I bet the same.

My nemesis won, but I had plenty more money. Sixty-three thousand three hundred, to be precise. Many rounds past. I had a six and a eight. The river was 2, 7, 9, 4, and 10. Lucky for me, my nemesis had wasted the last of his money on this round. You may think I lost, but put my cards and the River in order (besides the 2 and 4) and you get 6, 7, 8, 9, and 10. That was a flush! My nemesis had a pair, and flush beats a pair! *I had won!* I had the jewel! But wait. My nemesis! He wasn't a nemesis to just me, he was a nemesis to everyone!

The reason being: He was Amas in disguise!

So I shouted, "Hold it, buddy!" Amas flung around and his mask came off, and it was a revelation to everybody except for me.

"You!" Amas shouted.

"Wanna take this outside? But first…" I whistled as loud as I could and Dad, Kyle, Sammy, Bobby, Mary, Kim, and Roger came rushing up to see the scene.

We rushed went outside. Then, it was *on.*

92

Chapter XIV
Amas is Caught

DYLAN

Kyle was going to kick him, but, unfortunately, Amas had a jetpack strapped to his back. He flew up and Kyle missed.

"No fair! You have a jetpack just like FT-37 on *The Galactic Conflict!*" he said.

"Kyle, you watch way too much television." I said, and pulled out our jetpack. I flew up and jetted towards Amas.

Meanwhile, Marty said, "Are we gonna help him or not?"

"I don't know if we can while he's up – That's it!" Kyle threw two nearby fat sticks to me.

Then Kyle signaled, "Clog the jetpack with the sticks." Kyle almost missed, but Amas' sudden movement elevated the chance.

He had clogged the jetpack!

Amas had fallen at least fifteen feet from the ground. When Amas was 95% recovered, he awakened. There was police surrounding Amas. Chief Besmal was at the scene also.

"Well, you have made a slow recovery." he remarked. Amas couldn't fight back. As for right now, he's vulnerable.

"There's an important statement in Bayport's Bill of Rights and that statement is 'Always vote for justice!'" I said honorably.

"Mmph pafetuc mamumphel phizs kaphcot iphsmm. Mamphd tthosmph Phammer Phbomys dimdph phtimpth. " Amas muttered. It meant, "How pathetic that cadet is. And those Hamer Boys did it." (He was so weak, and he was groaning so much his words were not understandable)

The police sergeant forced Amas into the car. He was driven to headquarters, followed by Kyle and I.

In the car, I asked Kyle, "Can you believe it? We finally caught Amas."

"I know, it's amazing!" Kyle finished.

At police headquarters, Amas was locked up and the chief said, "He will be executed in a mere two weeks."

"Why two weeks?" I asked.

"Heck, we don't have the equipment! We do not buy our equipment before hand. Better yet, we don't buy it! We borrow it. But only if we need it." the chief answered, "And we need to find someone who has an execution chamber."

After that, we were a bit disappointed that Amas could not be executed today, but the bliss felling of Amas being caught overpowered the subject.

When we got home, I said, "Now if we can only get him to spit out a couple of confessions, we would be able to solve the mystery."

"I'm doubting he'll say anything at first." Kyle pointed out.

"Well, if all of us and Marty and the others go, we can maybe make him spit something out." I said.

So, with my solution, we went to police headquarters.

"So, Amas, we'll start out easy. Have you done any other burglaries besides at Aunt Sally's Fried Chicken, 3:45 am; Uncle Bob's Auto Shop, 4:15 am; Service Merchandise, 8:20 am; Price Low, 7:55 am; Del Champs, 11:43 am; William's Jewelry, 9:00; The Door Store, 5:34; The Bell Farm, 2:56; The Pizza Place, 4:22; and African Artifacts Museum and more from A-Z, 7:33?"

"Yes." Amas dozed.

"What's with him?" I asked Chief Besmal.

"We gave him a bit of truth serum before you got here." the Chief replied.

"Oh." I stammered.

"What other burglaries?" Kyle continued for me. Amas did not answer, but he handed a list from his jail cell to us. It had all of the burglaries he and his gang had done, (which was the sloppiest handwriting I had ever seen in my entire life, besides Dylan's), and that list looked like this:

Bulls-Eye Grocery Store, 3:29 am
The Most Popular Fashions in the Decade, 6:59 am
The Century's Shoe Place, 8:47 am
The Pizza Parlor, 4:44 am
Ancient Artifacts and Antiques, 10:37 am
The Flea Market, 8:34 am
Asian, African, and Chinese Products, 8:27 am
World's Most Famous People Museum, 6:39 am
The Children's Museum, 8:39 am

"Add that to the other list, and you get nineteen robberies in all!" I said.

"Question 3. Final question. Where is all of Adam Aksaw's money?" Kyle interrogated.

"Adam Aksaw's money is in a secret compartment in the - cough -, activated by the - cough -, closest to the compartment, switch to the - cough - on the - cough - of the cave 90 - cough - past the - cough - of the cave." Amas answered goofily. Then, the truth serum wore off. "Stupid me!" Amas shouted at himself. Then he slapped and punched himself.

"I think we oughta go." I whispered. Then we left. After dropping off the others, we decided to go to the cave.

"Ninety inches from the entrance." I repeated. Fortunately, Dad had brought his tape measure (he was on a meeting before knowing Amas had been caught) and measured ninety inches.

"Here!" I exclaimed when the tape measure had its end on ninety. There were six switches, and we flipped the third one to the left. Then a compartment lowered. You would not believe what we saw. *It was twenty-seven **million** one-dollar bills, piled in mountains and mountains! It felt like we were living in a dream!* (Mine anyway, because mine was living in gold and riches.)

Finally Kyle said something, "Wait a second. We cannot haul all of this money! Especially when crooks are roaming around."

"You're precisely right!" Dad said logically, "We need to bring the millionaire to the money, not the money to the millionaire."

So, we went to the millionaire's house and when he opened the door, he was surprised, "Boys! Albert! What are you doing here?"

"We found your money. Come on!" I said rapidly. He rushed to his limousine. We drove to the cavern, which the compartment stood open.

Personally, I thought he was not going to bother using the door. But he did. The driver was actually a bit enthusiastic, too. He hauled suitcases into the limousine carefully.

"I am not broke anymore!" Adam shouted to the world. When Marty heard of this revelation, he almost shouted, "What! You what!"

"We found Adam's money." I stammered purposely.

"One million dollars in one dollar bills?" Marty exclaimed after he had heard the whole story.

"*Twenty-seven* million, but close enough, and a one hundred percent chance of being over twenty-six million!" I corrected.

"Twenty-seven million!" Marty said, "Why, we have got to celebrate for this revelation!"

"Well, I could use a break in mystery solving, so, party it is!" Kyle shouted.

"Wait, first let's check on Amas." I said, "He could have escaped."

"Dylan's right. He's a tough criminal, all right." Marty warned. So, after seeing if Amas was still in headquarters, we grabbed Mary to help us make party preparations.

An hour later, the party was ready. We phoned Sammy, Kim, Roger, Bobby, the millionaire, Chief Besmal, even some police officers, and a few other friends (which were inexperienced at crime stopping) to join. We partied for a while before we got drinks.

Then, the millionaire said proudly, "I would like to propose a toast to Kyle, Dylan, and Albert Hamer for finding my money, and for putting Amas in jail." Most others were shocked.

I knew what they were thinking. 'They found Adam's money?' I glanced at Marty. He winked.

Then cake was next. I could say it was like a miniature party, without the presents and party favors. Before we knew it, the party was over.

"Time flies by when you're having fun." I sighed, commenting on the saying. Next, it was dinnertime. Since Aunt Denise wasn't cooking for all nine - Dad, Dylan, Sammy, Kim, Bobby, Roger, Chief Besmal, the millionaire, and I - of us (not including Ms. Hardy and herself), we ate at Marty's house. We had chicken and sausage gumbo, Marty's favorite. And for dessert, it was more cake.

"So, how did you find the compartment when he coughed on all of the important stuff?" Chief Besmal asked me.

"Context." I replied, finishing off my chocolate cake heartily.

"I believe you're actually doing better than your father." Chief Besmal remarked. That statement brought back memories, which I was now starting to remember when Dad worked for the New York police headquarters.

"Well, I'm off to work!" Dad would say every morning to my mom at 7:00.

"Okay, honey!" Mom would reply from the kitchen, making breakfast.

Then Mom would shout to us, "Breakfast is ready!"

"Be right there!" I'd answer, running toward the kitchen table. Kyle would walk formally to the table, the exact opposite of me.

I would groan. "Mom, why do we always have eggs benedict?"

"Because it has protein, calcium, vitamins, minerals, and water, also carbohydrates." Mom would answer adequately.

"Always puts things the logical way." I would murmur.

Suddenly there was a snapping noise, and I woke to life.

"What were you thinking about?" Marty questioned.

"When me and Kyle were about eight." I said embarrassingly.

"Anyway, when do you think this Amas thing will be over?" the millionaire said.

"About three weeks, Mr. Aks" --then the millionaire interrupted -- "Please, call me Adam. It is the least I can do."

"Anyway three weeks."

"Why three?" Adam asked, disagreeing.

"The police station has to get an execution chamber, and that takes a lot of money and time." I answered.

"Well, we can shoot Amas. Guns on me." Adam suggested, adding a raise to compliment the situation, and it was almost impossible to disagree.

"Alright." Chief Besmal said. On the way to the gun shop, something drastic occurred. Amas' gang appeared on the street, and almost rammed us into the ditch, but we stopped him and their plan reversed.

Finally, we arrived at the gun store. I got a rifle, Kyle got a machine gun, Dad got a bee-bee gun, and everyone else got blasters.

Then we arrived in shock at police headquarters, including the millionaire and Chief Besmal.

Amas had vanished!

Chapter XV
Amas' Freedom

KYLE

"Officers Miller, Tidwell, and Dunsworth, report to police headquarters' entrance immediately!" Chief Besmal's voice rang in the intercom speakers everywhere. Three men in uniform appeared from around a corner.

"Where is criminal seven million, three hundred eighty-nine thousand, two hundred sixteen?" Chief Besmal asked critically.

"I donno, I was working on the rash of car-stealing." Tidwell said stupidly.

"Do *not* talk to me in that tone of voice!" the chief scolded. Then Dunsworth and Miller pointed to Tidwell.

"Same." Dunsworth confessed. Chief Besmal sighed as he sat down at his rather large podium.

"Boys, Albert, you'll have to catch him again." he said glumly, then overreacted and shouted, "What is the meaning of this!" The voice yelled into the intercom.

The guard to Amas' cell, just awakening by the shout, said wearily, "Do you mind?"

His voice trailed off into a whimper when he saw that the chief was the one to shout. Luckily, Chief Besmal ignored him. But the fact that he was the one who let him escape would not slip his mind. And the overreaction was not over.

"You're the one who let Amas out?!" Chief Besmal's voice sounded like it was going through the intercom, but it wasn't.

"Imagine what it would be like if it was going through the intercom." I whispered to Dylan. Since the chief wasn't finished fussing, he did not hear.

All I heard was the last sentence: "You're fired!!"

I felt bad for the guy, so I said, "No, let him keep the job. Just give him severe punishments, like, um, no raises for a year, and he gets paid one hundred dollars less." I sorted out.

"That seems fair. But I'll have to check the laws about it." Chief Besmal stated. I was confused. He mulled the laws over.

"Article 2, Section 4, Part 1: The President, Vice President, and all civil officers of the United States shall be removed from office on impeachment for, and conviction of treason, bribery, or other high crimes or misdemeanors. Nope. Okay." Then he turned to the officer.

"You heard the consequences. And also, I will have a new guard. You will be the assistant guard." Stealthily, we exited headquarters.

"Oh, man! How are we supposed to catch him now? He's probably got a new name, hiding place, address..." the list was endless. Then, a white blur was spotted in the greenery.

It was not a plant. "Wait!" Dylan shouted suddenly. Dad skidded to a stop at the side of the road.

"There is a paper back in the grass!" Dylan continued. So, we backed up, and, thirty seconds later, looking at a sheet of torn paper. It was torn into half, with the other half missing. It didn't have all of the information, but here's what the paper said:

Collin Wae
592-1055 Misso

"Amas wrote this!" I said out loud, astonished.

"How do you know? It's as good as another person's letter." Dylan rejected.

"Well, Kyle you're right. It definitely needs verification. But it could be someone else, according to Dylan." Dad evened.

After dropping everyone off, we went home. We compared notes between the former note and previous notes. It was definite that the letter was Amas's.

"And there's only one street that starts with m-i-s-s-o. Missouri Street. 1055 Missouri Street." I discovered.

"The phone book is convenient. 1055 Missouri Street's phone number is: 592-1684. And a Collin Adams lives there." Dylan concluded.

"Then the w-a-e must be his phony middle name!" I almost shouted. Then we were tempted to go to 1055 Missouri Street, so we did with Dad's permission.

100

After riding the distance of at least 8 miles, we parked our bikes on the pavement of the asphalt road. Then we slithered through the green grass, cautious with every pace. Then at the side of the house in which Amas was hiding out in, a loud 'Got you!' filled the silenced air with alarm.

I recognized the voice immediately. The voice was Amas's! I heard no more, for two of Amas' henchmen tied and gagged us expertly. Then I believe another guy drugged us with sleepy juice and antidepressants (which made us forget everything).

When we awakened, we were in Amas's backyard hideout twenty feet away from each other.

"Where are we?" I questioned incoherently.

"I don't know, for pete's sake! They drugged me, too, you know." Dylan said.

"Well they drugged me first. I didn't know that they drugged you, too." I said.

"Duh!" Dylan said with a temptation to say that his brother was coo-coo.

"Let's use the pocketknife. My hands throb me unpleasantly." I said after one minutes time. Dylan tossed and seesawed his pocketknife, and finally got it out. He bladed through the tight knot, then slithered across the green grass to me. Dylan cut my knot.

"I've been thinking… and I have a plan: It's about time for their pizza. I heard one of the henchmen ordering it. We ring the doorbell. They think it's the pizza. They open the door. We beat 'em up and get them knocked out." I said, familiarizing the plan to Dylan immediately.

We put our plan into action. We knocked, they thought it was the pizza. They opened the door and we said simultaneously, "Knuckle sandwiches at your service!"

Then we pounded everyone in the house. Then, we escaped. After telling Dad, we got a plan… because we needed to wrap the case up… before we get hurt… or else…

Chapter XVI
The Last Battle

DYLAN

We explained the plan: Sneak up. Beat up. Police. Interrogation. Case closed. There was only one exclusion. They could be armed and prepared. But, to cover up, we called many reinforcements (which was the whole Army [which was about 175,000 people]) and Amas did not have a chance now. Five hours later, the Army arrived in formation. Marty was actually scared, and they were on our side! We marched over to the house.

Amas' men were not scared, for 175,000 of their reinforced robots were there, Level 2s only. This battle was getting to be bloodthirsty. The Army began to shoot and the robots started moving quickly. Kyle, Dad, and I modified our position silently towards Amas.

They were going to have a personal battle with him. The battle score was against us. Amas' robots were winning over the Army. We tripped Amas onto the cement driveway. He did not flinch.

He fisted Dad in the vertex of the head. He flew backwards about five inches, then landed with a '*thump*' on the cement. Thank Goodness he's not knocked out, but probably unable to fight.

"Get Dad to first-aid! An Army always comes with first-aid! I'll hold Amas off!" I panicked, but Kyle didn't blame him. This was a brave job for me to do, but Kyle didn't protest.

We needed to get Dad to help – fast, and we needed to get Amas to the police. The only option was to split up. Kyle dropped Dad off at the first aid section of the Army, after explaining the incident, of course. Then he ran back to help me. In the middle of the distance, he must have thought, no, better yet, knew something.

He had the element of surprise on his side. Kyle ran and got a square shot in the stomach. He slid across the driveway, and we had time. Time was the keyword.

We punched Amas in the stomach simultaneously. Kyle gasped when he noticed that there was 50 army men and 100 robots left. I had knocked out Amas when he poked me on the shoulder.

"What?" I said sassily. He pointed. I noticed that the nurse was dead, too, so I pointed in that direction. Kyle collapsed (until I caught him before he needed a nurse, which was unavailable) backwards when he saw the sight.

We ran over to Dad. He had gained consciousness, and looked a lot better.

"Fracture in the skull." Dad mulled, "How am I ever going to get near Denise without her freaking out?"

After discussing, I peered back at the battle. "Holy smoke!!!" 5 vs. 25! The Army was dead. 4, 3, 2... It decreased to two when a army tank took the robots and Amas' henchmen sinking to the driveway. Then, the police arrived.

They threw (and *really* threw) Amas into the police car, and we took another car.

Time for Step 4... Interrogation...

Chapter XVII
The Tables Turned

KYLE

Amas was conscious when we approached the police station. "I will not speak!" he declared.

"I will not!" The chief ignored him. When they arrived, they literally catapulted Amas in to the iron cell.

I said, "Give it up. "We have got your friends here, so you are hopeless."

"Oh, you are right. I might as well when my death is approaching."

"Death! A better word would be euthanasia or at least dissolution, but, my Lord, not death!" Aunt Denise shrieked.

"Whatever." Amas mumbled. "Anyway," – Adam interrupted, shouting, "Where's the rest of my money?"

"Huh?" Everyone said simultaneously. "There's more money. I did not want to tell you because it would put more pressure on you." Adam said.

"It is at the Nevada Casino of all Casinos." Amas confessed.

"*What!!*" Adam screamed, "I want a charter plane to Nevada – and I want it free!" He ran out of the station.

"Okay, to burglaries. Where is the stuff you stole at Aunt Sally's Fried Chicken at 3:45?" I asked.

"Secondary hideout at 746 Centre Street (these are what Amas names his hideouts)."

"Uncle Bob's Auto Shop at 4:15?" Dylan catechized.

"Madawaska." Amas answered.

"Service Merchandise, Price Low, and Del Champs?" Dad challenged.

"Third hideout." Amas answered, "Madawaska, first, third, second, third."

"Bull's Eye…" I made him continue.

"Madawaska." Amas sighed, "Madawaska, second, first, Madawaska, third, third, second, Madawaska, Madawaska."

"Execute." Dad said. They moved Amas to the chamber.

"WAIT!! One more thing. The diamond ring belongs to Adam, so let it go." I said.

Then, Amas was electrocuted. After that, we had an *enormous* party.

There were cakes, lots of them, for the entire police force was there.

"Well, boys, you have done it again and I hope you keep doing it at this rate, so you can be even better detective than your Dad! Not that I am insulting you, Albert." Chief Besmal stated.

Dad said, "I know. I'm proud of them, too!"

www.ingramcontent.com/pod-product-compliance
Lightning Source LLC
Chambersburg PA
CBHW051928240626
47153CB00004B/1419